Lo, How a Rose

The Nativity Story

J.R. SIMMONS

Published by:
Magic Unleashed Publishing.

MAGICUNLEASHED

This is a work of historical fiction. Although many names, characters, places, and incidents are real, the details of the story is the product of the author's imagination. This story was derived from accounts given in the New Testament. The goal is to give readers the opportunity to reflect on the true meaning of Christmas.

Paperback Edition:

ISBN-10: 1944137025
ISBN-13: 978-1-944137-02-1

ACKNOWLEDGEMENTS

A special thanks to my wife, Staci, for always being willing to make time for my crazy ventures.

Thanks to Kit Sealy for working through my fevered requests for updates and producing a fantastic, original cover. Thanks to Eileen Whitehead for painting a masterpiece nativity scene for the second version of the cover.

Thanks to Mikey Brooks for the wonderful separators and chapter images.

Thanks to Juli Caldwell for her continued editing support and being the expert in all things.

Thanks to Monique Bucheger for the read through and great insights and helping me lift my writing to the next level.

Thanks to you for reading this trying to make Christmas a little more meaningful.

DEDICATION

For my dad, Doug Simmons. Thank you for making the Christmas story come alive for me each and every year.

For my mom, Cindy Simmons. Thank you for always making Christmas a magical season.

Lo, How A Rose E'er Blooming

Lo, how a rose e'er blooming,
From tender stem hath sprung.
Of Jesse's lineage coming,
As men of old have sung;
It came, a flow'ret bright,
Amid the cold of winter,
When half spent was the night.

Isaiah 'twas foretold it,
The Rose I have in mind,
With Mary we behold it,
The virgin mother kind;
To show God's love aright,
She bore to men a Savior,
When half spent was the night.

German Christmas Hymn

PROLOGUE

NOAH

Noah squinted out over his fields attempting to identify the winged creatures gliding low over his vineyards. He willed his tired eyes to see more than the shadows he had become accustomed to. It seemed old age was finally catching up with him. With a resigned chuckle, Noah leaned down to the young boy standing next to him.

"Look there, Seth. Can you tell me what those birds are?"

It was a game that Noah enjoyed playing with his great-grandchildren. When he first noticed his sight fading, he decided to use their eyes as his own. The little ones loved spotting the birds and were always eager to identify them. If they did not know the names, the children would describe characteristics until Noah guessed the animal in question.

Birds had come to hold a special place in Noah's heart ever since that unforgettable day when a beautiful dove placed an olive leaf in his hand. He often found himself gazing at the sky overhead, mesmerized by the way the winged creatures flew through the skies, effortlessly remaining aloft as they circled over his vineyards. On more than one occasion, he imagined what it would be like to see the earth from their perspective.

"They are medium-sized, Grandfather. The color of their body is mostly light gray and they have dark gray wings. They look like ..." The small boy's face wrinkled in concentration as he studied the birds. "Pigeons!" Seth exclaimed excitedly. "They're pigeons! Do you think it could be the same flock that we saw yesterday?"

"I don't know, Seth," the old man replied. "It's possible, but there are an awful lot of pigeons out there."

At least there are now, the old man thought as he tried to make out the dim shapes circling above. *It's hard to believe that not so long ago, there were only seven.* As he continued watching the shadowy images of the birds, memories of the great flood wanted to play through the aging prophet's mind. Rather than give in to them, Noah gave himself a mental shake and pushed the unwanted memories back into the recesses of his mind. The time with his grandchildren was too precious, and he would not spend it worrying about what once had been. Studying the young boy, he winked slyly.

"Then again, they could be the same. Maybe they are coming back to say hello to you, boy. After all, not many would have recognized that they were pigeons from this distance."

Peering up at his grandfather's face, Seth pushed his lower lip out, "Grandfather," he pouted. "I think you are teasing me."

"Would I do that to my favorite grandson, Seth?" Noah feigned an expression of sincerity. When Seth's pout remained firmly in place, Noah broke into a wheezing laugh.

Seth appeared momentarily offended, but the old man's laughter must have been contagious because, after a moment, a sheepish smile broke through the pout. With a callused hand, Noah patted the youth's head. The boy was a treasure, and Noah relished the time that they spent together in the fields, away from everything else and the distractions of home.

Of all Noah's grandchildren, Seth enjoyed bird watching the most. When he wasn't working in the fields with his father or playing with his friends, Seth spent his time studying the magnificent creatures with the old prophet. After a few months' tutelage, he had learned the names of many. The boy's sharp eyesight caught details that escaped all but a few of the other children. For this reason, Noah found himself looking forward to Seth's visits more than most, so they could wander to the outer edges of the vineyards and enjoy the fascinating animals together.

Once the pigeons disappeared into the horizon, Noah turned his gaze to what remained of the sun. It sank low behind the mountains and the picture it painted overhead nearly took his breath away. A myriad of different shades of orange laced the sky and emphasized the outline of the clouds dotting the heavens. As old as Noah was, he still marveled at the beauty God continually placed before his aging eyes. Knowing that the young boy would appreciate the vista for what it was, Noah tapped the boy's shoulder and pointed.

"Seth," he whispered quietly. "Isn't it beautiful?"

The awed look in the boy's eyes, and the way he slipped his small hand into Noah's own, told the old man that his assumption had been correct. The boy was indeed a treasure. Noah was grateful that Seth was still innocent enough to enjoy the natural beauty of a simple sunset. Soon enough his interests would be pulled away by work, education, and girls. For now, however, he remained heartwarmingly innocent. In moments like these, Noah realized how blessed he truly was.

They shared a moment of quiet contemplation, caught in the magnificence of the sunset, before Noah finally nudged the lad and began the short walk home. Seth would occasionally dart off of the path and return with a feather, sometimes exotic, sometimes commonplace, but he would always return with the same expression of excitement on his young face. Each time Noah would carefully examine the object of interest and compliment Seth on his find. He knew the boy was collecting the feathers, and he couldn't think of a better hobby for his sharp-eyed grandson.

Strolling up to the small house that he shared with his wife, Noah saw that Seth's mother and father were waiting for him. They waited on a crude wooden bench near the front door speaking in low voices with his wife, Naamah.

As the old man and the young boy neared, Seth's mother rose to her feet. "Seth, are you ready?" she asked. "We have much to do tomorrow, and we will be waking early."

Seth ran to her and showed her the newest additions to his collection. "Look, Mama, I found all of these on our walk back to the house."

Obviously interested, she bent down to study the feathers. "Doesn't that black one belong to a raven?"

Noah smiled to himself. Seth's mother had been one of his more enthusiastic bird watchers in her youth.

"I think so, Mama. I can't wait to add it to my collection! Are we leaving now?"

"Yes, Seth. Give your grandfather and grandmother a hug and thank them for letting you visit."

Seth flung his arms around Noah's neck and held on tight. "Thank you, Grandfather! I had a wonderful time. I hope we can go out again, soon."

"Of course, Seth," Noah replied. "Now hurry home and get some sleep. You won't be any use to your father in the morning if you stay up too late."

Seth hurried to hug his grandmother, and then the young family started toward their home.

Naamah smiled at Noah. "You do realize you are stealing all of my grandchildren, don't you? They always forget I am here after returning from one of your walks."

He grinned, "I have no doubt that you will win him back just as soon as your next loaf of bread comes out of the oven."

With a loving chuckle, Naamah took Noah by the hand and led him into the house, where his dinner waited on the table.

Later that night, Noah sighed as he limped into the small room he shared with his wife. Though supper had been wonderful, his legs and hips ached from the strain of the afternoon stroll. When he reached the foot of his sleeping mat, Noah lowered himself slowly until he was able to sit.

"I'm not as young as I used to be Naamah," he said, gingerly lifting one leg so he could rub away the dull pain.

"You've been saying that a lot lately," Naamah teased. "Now leave that leg alone. Get back up and change into your nightclothes. I will massage it for a moment before we blow out the candles."

With a grateful smile, he obediently stood to change before hurrying back, anxious to slide under the warmth of the heavy woolen blanket. True to her word, Naamah sat at the foot of his mat and kneaded the tightened muscles, working them loose as she chattered amiably about the happenings of the day. When she finished the massage, she crawled over to her own sleeping mat beside her husband's. Noah sat up drowsily. He leaned over to thank his wife and give her a quick peck on the cheek before closing his weary eyes and drifting off to sleep.

As Noah stood in the giant wooden entryway of the ark, tears streamed down his cheek, mixing with the first raindrops that fell from the swollen clouds above. He had worked so hard to warn the people of their wickedness. He tried to teach them of the goodness of God and what awaited them if they continued in their current path of spiritual destruction. His instruction had been met with scorn, mocking laughter, and at times, physical violence. The people had rejected his message and in so doing they had also rejected their Creator.

Noah clearly remembered the damning revelation as though it were yesterday, the all-powerful voice he heard telling him that the opportunity for instruction was at an end. The depravity and wickedness of the human race had reached an unalterable state, and the time for action had arrived. Where once his days had been spent calling the people to repentance, Noah was now commanded to build an ark and fill it with animals, at least two of every kind. God provided him exact instructions as to dimensions of the ship and how he must build it.

Building the ark had been a challenge, not only for Noah, but for his family as well. They endured the jeers and taunts of their neighbors throughout the construction and loading of the animals. Noah and his family had been forced to take turns standing guard over the giant boat to protect it from many of the more destructive and malicious individuals. They prayed often for continued support and strength, not only to finish the ark, but to withstand the abuse they took from those they once considered friends.

As difficult and demanding as the work had been to build and populate the ark, it was nothing compared to when the first raindrops fell. Now Noah could only look on sadly as a few of the bystanders shouted in dismay before being scorned to silence by the rest. Most of the people were more abusive than before, hurling insults, rotten fruit, and even stones at the hard-working family as they made their final preparations. Fighting back the despair, Noah turned from the condemned men and women for the last time as he shuffled into the large boat. With a silent gesture, he signaled for his sons to pull in the large plank and close the massive door.

Not long after Noah and his family entered the ark, the scoffing mob was driven back to their homes by the fierceness of the storm. Wiping the backs of his hands over his swollen eyes, Noah instructed his sons to verify that the animals were secure one last time before asking his family to join him. They quickly went about their tasks, rushing to and fro on the different levels of the massive ship.

"Everything will be all right, Noah," Naamah assured him, sliding a comforting arm around his waist. "We have done everything the Lord commanded. He will not forsake us in our time of need."

Feeling his throat tighten, Noah nodded. Together, they silently waited for the children and their spouses to return, listening as the rain pounded against the dark hickory planks of the ark, echoing loudly on the bulky wooden frame. When the family returned from their chores, Noah urged them all to kneel. In heartfelt prayer, the patriarch pleaded with God for protection from the upcoming storm and the strength to face the terrors ahead.

Over the furious storm and the panic of the animals, Noah could hear that many people had returned. They banged on the side of the ark, begging and screaming to be let in. When they realized they pleaded in vain, violent weeping and angry threats replaced the begging. Because he knew that soon he would no longer be heard over the commotion, Noah commanded his family to continue in personal prayer. Kneeling, he tried to shut out the shouts of terror.

Outside, rain pounded the ark, beating against the solid outer frame of the ship. The shouts and shrieks intensified briefly before fading as people were carried away and lost in the full fury of the storm. Feeling utterly helpless, Noah did the only thing that he could think of. With tears streaming down his grizzled cheeks to soak into his thick beard, he continued to pray.

"Open the doors, Noah!" someone shouted in terror. "We are sorry. We believe you about the flood! Please let us in!"

Turning away from the frantic voice, Noah tried to concentrate on his prayers within the ark, but no matter what he did, he couldn't shut out the terrified shrieks.

Suddenly Ham jumped to his feet. "I have to open the doors, Papa! All of those people are going to die!"

"No!" Noah barked hoarsely, feeling the strain in his voice. "If you open the doors, we will all die! The Lord has commanded that the doors remain closed. Those people have been warned countless times, but they would not cease in their debauchery! This is God's punishment! It is neither our right nor our place to interfere." He took a deep breath and tried to regain a portion of his composure, "Son, please. We are now at His mercy. It is only through the Lord's will and the strength of our faith that we will live through this cleansing. Adhere to His holy council, because now more than ever, our lives depend on strict obedience."

Ham glared angrily at Noah, but his fury was no match for his father's grim determination. Finally, the younger man looked away and slowly dropped to his knees. Noah's eyes followed his son. When he saw Ham kneel, he also knelt with his family and continued his prayer.

As the sounds of the storm outside intensified, the screams diminished until all Noah heard was the sound of the flood water slamming into the sides of the ark and the wailing wind rattling the weathered, wooden panels.

A sweet, melodic voice jerked him from his nightmare. "Noah."

The gut-wrenching terror he had experienced seconds earlier melted away to be replaced with a tranquility he knew well. Warmth showered over him as if Noah had stepped into sunlight after a long and dreary winter.

Basking in the love that only the Spirit of God could bring, Noah listened to the words of his Lord, the deity he had devoted his entire life to serving.

"Noah, my faithful son, thou hast served me well, and it is time that I reveal thy next calling unto thee. I know the horror of the cleansing continues to worry thee. Thou shalt be called to share a message of joyful tidings such as this world hath never known. I have chosen thee, Noah. Thou shalt proclaim the birth of my forerunner, John, to a certain person whom I shall make known unto thee at a later time. Thou shalt also reveal the news of *my* birth unto others, whom I shall also make known unto thee. Thou shalt tell the world of the birth of Jehovah, its Savior. When the time cometh to reveal this knowledge to the world, thou shalt be known unto the world as Gabriel."

CHAPTER 1

ZACHARIAS

With a muted groan, Zacharias sat up and rubbed his eyes. Even after a full night's rest, his body ached from the time he spent on the road. The journey from Hebron to Jerusalem grew longer each time he made it. Sighing inwardly, Zacharias pushed back his thin blanket and sat up. He stretched deeply, raising his hands over his head and extending his legs in an effort to wake up his aching muscles.

"I really ought to move closer to the city," he muttered as he pushed himself to his feet. He reached out a steadying hand to a small stand holding a basin of water near his sleeping mat.

As he said it, he knew that such a move could never happen. He liked the village of Hebron. More to the point, if he ever so much as mentioned the idea to his wife, she would lock herself in their home and refuse to come out. Elisabeth loved their house. She constantly added homey touches to give it an ever more welcoming air. He would sooner scrub the floors of the priests' living quarters on hands and knees than attempt to persuade Elisabeth to abandon their small home in the hill country of Judah.

He quickly washed his bearded face with a wet washcloth before groping blindly for the towel sitting on the stand. After grasping it, Zacharias wiped away the excess water.

"Are you coming, Uncle?" asked a voice from the hall.

Recognizing the speaker as his nephew, Aaron, Zacharias grunted in answer and shuffled unhurriedly to the entryway. The boy was new to temple service, and he still turned to Zacharias for guidance. Zacharias took one look at the youth's scraggly beard and earnest face with a shake of his head.

"We must hurry," Aaron said anxiously. "They are going to cast lots soon and you are going to make us late."

"Relax, Aaron," Zacharias said amiably, stepping back into his quarters. "I have worked in the temple longer than you have been alive and I have yet to miss a casting."

When Aaron threw an anxious glance over his shoulder, Zacharias sighed again. The boy worried continually about the most inconsequential things. Not wanting to add to his nephew's concern, he removed his sleeping robe and changed into his temple clothing. He ran his fingers through his hair and beard, grateful that Elisabeth was not there to chide him about his appearance. With a final flourish, he put the white priest's mitre on top of his head.

"I was just trying to get the aches out," he said, falling into step beside the much younger priest. "I am an old man, after all, and the road to Jerusalem isn't as easy as it used to be."

"It isn't all that far, Uncle," Aaron teased. "You are just getting soft."

Zacharias grunted sourly. "You tell me that in fifty years, boy. One day you will grow old as well, and your bones will ache from long journeys. Then you tell me that 'it isn't all that far.'"

As they strode out of the temple living quarters and toward the inner sanctums where the officiating priests gathered each morning, a few of the other priests called out greetings to Zacharias. He smiled and waved as each person called his name. He had worked in the temple for a long time. While he either knew or was related to many of them in one way or another, he noticed a few new faces.

Zacharias shuffled forward, slowing his pace as he studied the skilled workmanship of the temple. Although some sections of the holy edifice were still under construction, the beauty of magnificent architecture still took his breath away. The glory of the house of the Lord overwhelmed him and he stopped, satisfied to simply drink in the site and spirit of the glorious structure.

"Zacharias!" called a priest from across the courtyard, interrupting his musings. "How is Elisabeth?"

"She is doing well, thank you. Spending way too much of her time in that flower garden of hers, if you ask me!" Zacharias answered.

He turned to Aaron and dropped his voice. "Do you know that man? I recognize his face, but for the life of me, I can't place his name."

Aaron shook his head. "Well, you have been here a long time. You must have talked with him at some point." He smiled. "By his greeting, I assume that wives came up during the course of your conversations."

With a frown, Zacharias scratched his chin. "Apparently so," he muttered absently. Then he shrugged. "There are too many priests around here, my boy. I can't keep track of them anymore. Good thing he was too far away for a prolonged conversation."

Aaron laughed. "You used to be able to remember their names. I suppose you really are getting old."

Zacharias quirked a questioning eyebrow, but Aaron was already falling in with the group of priests who gathered for the casting. Without knowing quite why, Zacharias felt a twinge of excitement as he followed his nephew. Not even the sour smell of men in heavy clothes sweating in the morning sun could dampen his enthusiasm. Something deep within told him that today would be different than a standard day of service.

Joining the queue of priests, he intertwined his fingers as he waited for his turn to cast lots. It had been some time since his last visit to the inner sanctum of the temple. For some reason, however, Zacharias felt an increased desire to burn incense in the Holy Place today. Not wanting to face disappointment, he tried to dismiss the feeling. There were many priests in attendance, and the chances of him being selected were extremely small. He knew that he would most likely end up performing animal sacrifices at the bronze altar or serving in one of the many cleaning assignments that befell most of the priests.

Each day, before the men of God went about their normal temple duties, they participated in an unbiased selection method to determine who would burn incense at the altar in the Holy Place. The winner's only task was to enter the sacred room and throw the perfumed powder on the designated altar at sunrise and sunset. It was a simple job, and the fortunate priest was permitted to enter a portion of the temple that was off limits under normal circumstances. While the priest was within the sacred room, parishioners would wait in prayer for the smoke of the incense to rise. Following that, the priest would exit the Holy Place and pronounce a benediction, thus concluding the blessed ritual.

Long ago, the Lord had revealed that the scent of incense was pleasing unto him. For many years, only the High Priests had been permitted to perform the task, so when it became available to all of the descendants of Aaron, all who worked in the temple coveted the assignment. Due to the large number of priests vying for the privilege, they would cast lots to decide. Each individual desiring consideration would write their name on a potsherd and drop it into a basket. When all names had been entered, a designated authority then mixed up the broken pieces of pottery and yet another would pull out a name. Through this method, the opportunity was opened to all priests, and no one could be accused of taking the honor unjustly. It was also generally accepted that the Lord could take a hand in the casting if He so chose.

Usually, Zacharias was satisfied to serve wherever assigned, and he was a bit surprised to find how much he wanted his potsherd to be chosen. He waited patiently as the others tossed their tokens into the basket, knowing that each silently hoped that the privilege might fall to them. The line moved swiftly, and it was not long before Aaron shuffled aside, allowing Zacharias to step up and cast his lot. He dropped his personalized potsherd in with the rest and moved out of the way. Standing next to Aaron, he tried to convince himself of the odds and tell himself that if only one priest were to be selected, the chances of his winning were next to impossible. However, the strange sense of anxiety still filled him as he waited for the others to finish. Without knowing why, he closed his eyes and uttered a silent prayer.

Moments later, he felt an elbow dig him in the ribs. "Uncle!" Aaron hissed. "Look!"

Zacharias opened his eyes and blinked. In the midst of his concentration, he had not realized that all of the lots had been cast. He glanced over to where Aaron pointed and saw that the presiding priest was beaming at him openly while holding up his potsherd. He had been chosen! Zacharias opened his mouth to say something, but no sound came out. The tingle of excitement was replaced by an unexplainable feeling of euphoria.

"Looks like you have an easy day ahead of you," Aaron teased as the other priests dispersed, a few of them muttering in disappointment. "Congratulations, my friend. I must go, for I have tasks of my own. I'll see you at dusk."

Zacharias nodded, still unable to speak. He watched as the young men strode away, the enthusiasm and vigor of youth in every step. There would be many petitioners this day, and they all knew the importance of staying on top of their daily chores. Zacharias knew that he should prepare for the morning burning, but he wanted a moment to ponder what had happened. He found a secluded bench and sat down to think. Never before had he felt the need to pray during a casting. He possessed a firm testimony of God and had always been content to leave the casting of lots in God's perfect hands. *Why did I feel that particular desire today?*

He thought of other prayers he had voiced to the Lord and the answers he had received. Then, as was unavoidable whenever his mind explored this particular line of thought, he turned to the one prayer that had been voiced over and over. It was the one answer that perplexed him still. As he grew older, the reply made no more sense to him than it had while he was still in his youth.

Not long after he married Elisabeth, the pair of them fervently prayed to have a child. The answer they both felt after their prayers was a feeling that they should just be patient. When Elisabeth continued to age without conceiving, this answer became increasingly bewildering. At times he wondered if he could have misinterpreted the response, but then he would receive an answer to another prayer, like he had today, and the feeling of peace that passed over him would reinforce the reply he had received so long ago.

As his thoughts turned back to burning incense in the afternoon, he couldn't stop a silly grin from lighting up his face. *Wait until I tell Elisabeth.*

"Zacharias," a young priest said hesitantly, "I do not mean to disturb you, but the petitioners are already gathering outside of the temple gates. There is still much to prepare before we can receive them."

"Yes, yes of course. I am on my way," said Zacharias, rising to his feet. "I apologize for the delay, my brother."

"There is no reason," the priest answered with an understanding smile. "It is an exciting day for you."

The morning burning passed uneventfully, but the faint buzz of excitement continued to fill him. Though the afternoon usually dragged for the priest in charge of burning the incense, the rest of the day passed quickly for Zacharias. As evening approached, exhilaration at the prospect that soon it would again be time to burn incense to his Lord filled him with the energy of a much younger man. He felt the importance in each and every chore he was assigned, no matter how tedious or repetitive. It was as though the casting breathed new life into his aging bones.

As he carefully measured the ingredients that would eventually form the batch of incense to be used once the current stock dwindled, he was surprised to notice that the aches from the previous day's journey were gone. When he finished with the incense, Zacharias found that the candle basket was low. He began to cut the new candles that would replace those currently residing on the menorah within the Holy Place. The priest who performed the burning's only other task within the Holy Place was to replace the burned down candles with fresh ones. He placed seven of the candles in the satchel he would take with him and refilled the basket containing the extras.

The sun continued its steady pace toward the horizon, and he felt his excitement grow. After what felt like ages, the glowing orb retreated and Zacharias could barely contain his pleasure. Attempting to compose himself, he made his way to a section of the temple where the animal sacrifices were made. Not wanting to rush the experience, he walked slowly, allowing it all to sink in. Gingerly, he threaded his way through the kneeling throngs of petitioners until he reached a small room containing the implements he would need. Though he had taken this path countless times in his years of service, this evening it felt different.

Reverently, Zacharias stepped up to the entrance of the restricted area. He walked past the bronze altar of sacrifice in the center of the court, quietly moving to a small room off to one side. As he walked, Zacharias considered what would happen once he finished burning the incense. He glanced back at the congregation of kneeling Jews, knowing they would continue with their prayers while he worked inside. Once the ritual was completed, he would exit the Holy Place and pronounce a blessing over them. Running through the words of the benediction in his mind, Zacharias tried to keep a firm grasp on them as nervousness threatened to wipe the prayer from memory.

Feeling peculiarly overwhelmed, he stopped before the laver, a great bronze bowl with large feet. Beyond the laver, an entrance led to the Holy Place where he would burn the incense. He carefully set down the satchel containing the candles and removed his temple shoes in preparation for the ceremonial cleansing of his hands and his feet.

Zacharias washed thoroughly, reflecting on the ritualistic cleansing and the symbolism behind it. The Lord required man to be completely spotless and free of sin in order to enter His presence. By commanding priests to wash before entering the Holy Place, the Lord reminded them of the need for spiritual purity and abstinence from sin.

Zacharias finished the cleansing and picked up his satchel. Stepping toward the entrance of the Holy Place, his hands began to shake slightly as his anxiety increased. *Something is about to happen! I can feel it!* When he entered the sacred room, rays of fading sunlight mixed with the candlelight and glinted off of the golden fixtures within. Drawing a steadying breath, Zacharias stepped all of the way in.

The Golden Altar of Incense stood in the middle of the room, the menorah to the left of the altar, and the table of shewbread to the right. Twelve pieces of shewbread, divided evenly into two stacks of six on the table, were topped off with a nugget of frankincense. The bread was still fresh, having been replaced the previous Sabbath. Upon the next Sabbath day, the priests would gather together in the Holy Place and partake of the sacred bread before replacing it with newly prepared shewbread.

The menorah candles were nearly spent. Before Zacharias could burn the incense, he would need to attend to the menorah. He studied it for a moment, his eyes traveling over the ornate base, up the stem, and over the seven branches, each holding the tiny remnants of a candle. Carefully, he reached into his satchel and pulled out a fresh stick of wax.

He removed one of the stubs on the menorah and replaced it with the new one. He made sure to light the fresh candle with the old before extinguishing and stuffing the remnant into the satchel. One by one, he switched out all of the candles on the Menorah. As he worked, he drank in the spirit of being in one of the most sacred rooms of the holiest edifice in the world.

When he finished, Zacharias turned to the center of the room. He slowly approached the golden altar. Made of acacia wood and overlaid with pure gold, it was beautifully crafted and easily the focal point of the Holy Place. The altar was long and square, standing nearly waist high. Four horns protruded from the top, one at each corner. Long, slender poles ran through rings on the front and back, providing a means for transporting the altar when necessary. Coals smoldered under a latticed grate, glowing red in the dim candlelight. Next to the gold altar rested a small container of powdered incense and a tiny incense boat. Reverently, Zacharias picked up the boat and filled it with the sweet-smelling powder. Praises of thanksgiving filled his soul as he poured it over the altar.

A wonderful smell wafted up. Zacharias closed his eyes and inhaled deeply, his heart leaping with gladness now that he had completed his task. He felt closer to his God than ever before, and he savored the feelings of joy and peace flooding through him. He still could not place the strange excitement he had felt all day, but if it were only so he could experience this moment, it was enough. His heart was full and his testimony was sated.

Through closed eyelids, Zacharias saw a brilliant flash of white. He forced them open. Astonishment flooded through him. He blinked, but still couldn't believe the scene before him. A man dressed in dazzling white stood to the right side of the altar. An even stronger light filled the area around him. When the being smiled, the white grew brighter still. Zaharias glanced back at the entrance and noticed it was undisturbed. Fear of unworthiness began to settle over him. His gaze caught God's holy messenger, an angel of the Lord.

Righteous authority emanated from the heavenly being in waves so powerful that Zacharias was certain if he stretched forth his hand, he might touch it. It pulsed through him, filling Zacharias with energy and light. The angel opened his mouth to speak. Awed by his visitor's holy presence, Zacharias dropped to a kneeling position. The gentle tone banished Zacharias' fear.

"Fear not, Zacharias: for thy prayer is heard; and thy wife Elisabeth shall bear thee a son, and thou shalt call his name John."

Zacharias gaped at the angel with his mouth open. Had he heard correctly? He would have a son? As he tried to comprehend the much desired news, the angel continued.

"And thou shalt have joy and gladness; and many shall rejoice at his birth. For he shall be great in the sight of the Lord, and shall drink neither wine nor strong drink; and he shall be filled with the Holy Ghost, even from his mother's womb. And many of the children of Israel shall he turn to the Lord their God. And he shall go before him in the spirit and power of Elias, to turn the hearts of the fathers to the children, and the disobedient to the wisdom of the just; to make ready a people prepared for the Lord."

The angel smiled at Zacharias as he finished the announcement, but Zacharias could only stare at the personage before him. *Elisabeth is going to bear a child? But that's impossible,* he thought to himself. They had both resigned themselves to the fact that her childbearing days had long passed. Before he stopped to think, a question slipped out. Though doubting in origin, it nonetheless carried the formal tone used in prayer and when speaking of sacred things.

"Whereby shall I know this? For I am an old man, and my wife well stricken in years."

As soon as the last word escaped his lips, Zacharias raised his hands over his mouth in horror. Here he stood in the Holy Place. A messenger of God came to him, and the first words out of his mouth were of doubt.

The angel fixed Zacharias with a stern expression and pointed his finger at him. "I am Gabriel, that stands in the presence of God; and am sent to speak unto thee, and to shew thee these glad tidings. And, behold, thou shalt be dumb, and not able to speak, until the day that these things shall be performed, because thou believest not my words, which shall be fulfilled in their season."

Zacharias opened his mouth to tell Gabriel he was sorry and beg for forgiveness, but no sound came out. He gazed at the angel and saw that his mouth was still moving, but Zacharias could not hear anything. Understanding flooded through him. Because of his doubts, Zacharias could no longer hear nor speak. He looked up as Gabriel, who smiled warmly at him despite the rebuke, mouthed something and disappeared.

Zacharias sat huddled on the floor, his mind a flood of giddy bewilderment. He gaped at the spot that Gabriel occupied only moments before and thought about the words that had been spoken to him. Gabriel said that Zacharias would have a son. *A son!* After all of this time, after all of the prayers he and his wife uttered, Zacharias and Elisabeth were going to experience the joy of having a child together.

A silly grin broke across Zacharias' face. It would not be just any child, but a child that would be — *how had Gabriel worded it?* — great in the sight of the Lord. His son would be filled with the spirit; he would bring many to God. He would make ready a people prepared for the Lord. *Make ready a people prepared for the Lord?*

The amused smile that lit Zacharias' face faltered. *The Lord is coming,* he thought to himself in stunned amazement. Zacharias was familiar with the scriptures. He knew that before the Lord would come to his people in the flesh, a forerunner would appear and prepare the way for him. His son would be the forerunner of the *Messiah?* Had the time arrived for the Lord to come and redeem all men? Zacharias had read accounts from the prophets hinting that time was short, but he never expected to be alive when it happened, let alone to father the forerunner.

Zacharias rose slowly to his feet, realizing that his task still lay unfinished. He still clutched the incense boat tightly in his hands, but the satchel had fallen to the floor. Some of the candles had slipped out. With shaking hands, he replaced the boat before reaching down and gathering up the fallen candles. Reverently, he placed them back in the satchel and stood.

Shuffling toward the door, he paused before opening it. The old man turned back one more time and studied the sacred room. It was the same as it had when he first entered, inviting and beautiful. At a glance, one would not gather that only moments ago a messenger of the Lord had been present. His gaze lingered on the dancing light of the candles. He could still smell the faint aroma of the incense. As he inhaled the fragrance once again, he wondered how he was going to finish the ritual now that he couldn't speak. Shaking his head in wonder at what he had witnessed, the elderly priest turned his back on the golden incense altar for the final time and exited the Holy Place.

Zacharias re-entered the court of the priests in time to see Aaron briskly walking toward him. As the boy approached, Zacharias watched his mouth move. He knew that the youth was trying to communicate, but the old priest could only hear the same silence which fell over him since Gabriel's final pronouncement. Zacharias pointed to his ears, then to his mouth and then he shook his head, trying to convey to Aaron the fact that he could not hear nor speak. Aaron stopped in front of him, and, observing him quizzically, he said something else. Zacharias shrugged to indicate that he did not understand and motioned to his ears and mouth again.

Zacharias smiled slightly, watching as comprehension slowly registered on his young relation's face. The boy pointed to Zacharias ears, then his mouth, then toward the door of the Holy Place. Zacharias watched intently and nodded. Then, unable to contain the wonderful message any longer, Zacharias pointed up to the sky, motioned toward the room he had just exited, and then to himself.

Aaron looked at him in astonishment. He pointed at Zacharias and then pointed toward the heavens. Zacharias smiled broadly and nodded, tears glistening in his eyes as Aaron pulled him into a rough embrace. After a moment, Aaron let go and pointed down toward the crowd of waiting people. He then pointed at the fading light of the sunset and then at the Holy Place, indicating that Zacharias had been inside for quite a long time. He turned and walked forward a few steps before pausing and motioning for Zacharias to follow him. Zacharias breathed a sigh of relief as he followed Aaron toward the waiting congregation. At least Aaron would be able to help him explain what had happened and why he could not offer the final prayer.

When Zacharias stepped off of the last step, he saw that Aaron was already preparing to speak to the crowd. Zacharias hurried over to younger priest and touched him on the shoulder, motioning that he would like to address the people first. He could see that the crowd was buzzing about this break from tradition. Zacharias could almost hear their unasked questions. Why had he taken so long in the Holy Place? Why wasn't he pronouncing the blessing? Some of them were pointing up at the Holy Place and then at him. A couple of people wore irritated expressions, but most watched him with curiosity.

Zacharias smiled at them and waited for all the mouths to quit moving. When he felt reasonably sure that he had their attention, he opened and closed his mouth to show them that he could no longer speak. He pointed up toward the heavens and then at the Holy Place. The crowd fell quiet and watched as Zacharias wordlessly explained that he had received a vision. When the old man felt that they understood, he moved away from the congregation and motioned to Aaron.

Aaron stepped up and concluded the evening prayer. Zacharias smiled gratefully as he watched. Exhaustion overwhelmed him, making him more than ready for a good night's rest. For the first time he could remember, he looked forward to the end of his ministration period so he could go home and share these glorious tidings with his wife.

CHAPTER 2

ELISABETH

E lisabeth glared at the empty honeypot with both fists planted on her hips. It was just like Zacharias to scrape the vessel clean and then return it without telling her. She had not planned on visiting the market until tomorrow, but now she would need to go and purchase more honey. *I should just wait and he can go without. It would serve him right,* she thought, even as she picked up the pot. If the worst a woman could say about her husband was that he left the honeypot empty … well, she knew many who put up with worse.

Ever since they married, Elisabeth had made a custom of serving Zacharias freshly baked bread with honey on his first night back from temple service. Her husband often said this was one of his favorite traditions, and she would not chance his returning to a honey-less house. She laughed as she thought of the sweet, gentle man. Zacharias had always been lavish in his admiration of her, and while his praise often brought a flush to her cheeks, she secretly loved it.

Elisabeth remembered back to those years when that loving support had meant everything to her. For so long she had wanted to present Zacharias with a child ... wanted equally to give herself a child. His patience and kind words were the only things that kept her from sinking into despair when depression threatened to overwhelm her as year after childless year passed.

With a quiet sigh of regret, Elisabeth turned from the shelf. Although Zacharias was not due to come back for a day or two, she had never been one to procrastinate when things should be done. After taking a brief inventory of her food stock, she made a quick mental list of what she needed to purchase. She made some calculations of what it should all cost and slipped the coins she would need into one of the pockets on her dress, adding a few extras, just in case. With a considering glance over her clothing selection, she quickly chose a scarf that would match and properly cover her hair. When she was ready, Elisabeth picked up the large basket she used for shopping and loaded it with the honeypot. She opened the front door, looking forward to the leisurely stroll through the marketplace.

As she walked passed her flower garden in front of the house, Elisabeth breathed in deeply, inhaling the fresh, earthy scent. She stopped to gaze lovingly at the beautiful arrangements that she spent so much time cultivating. It had not been easy in the hot temperature and dry climate, but with a lot of patience and time she had grown a beautiful garden full of life and color. Irises, lavender, tulips, and more were arranged to accent the roses they surrounded. With a smile, she reached out and stroked the soft velvety petals of one of the beautiful flowers. Roses had always been her favorite and it had taken quite some time to find what would grow and complement them the most.

Though her husband continued to believe that a child might one day be possible, she long ago resigned herself to the fact that she would not bear children. During that difficult time, Zacharias encouraged her to find something that might keep her mind occupied so that she wouldn't dwell on what was not meant to be. She tried a myriad of hobbies from cooking to weaving, but her heart had not been in it. One day, they took a stroll together in the countryside. He must have watched as she bent to examine some wildflowers. The very next time he returned from his temple duties, he brought back a wide assortment of seeds from the Jerusalem markets. Zacharias even helped her dig out a plot of ground in front of the house in preparation for her new flower garden. From that day forward, every time he came back from Jerusalem, he brought different seeds for her to experiment with.

He was such a thoughtful man, always proving his love in new and surprising ways. She thought about how lucky she was to have been promised to Zacharias. Elisabeth knew that many men divorced women who were unable to conceive and she could only guess at how often the counsel had been recommended to Zacharias. Yet he stood by her side all these years, refusing to hear of it. A filthy word, he always called it, and he would not allow it to be spoken in or around his home. She loved him so much for that kindness and dedication, so she worked hard to be a good wife for him, worthy of the love he had always shown her.

All of the sudden, she could not wait for him to come home. She knew that it would most likely be another day or so, but she wanted things to be ready for him. She moved quickly through the city streets, offering hurried greetings to friends and neighbors. Filled with a strange sense of urgency, she failed to negotiate as stringently as she had in the past. The result was that by the time her basket was full, her pocket containing the coins was nearly empty. For a moment, Elisabeth chided herself for her impatience, but in the end, excitement won out and she hurried home. She did not know why, but Elisabeth had a sudden suspicion that her husband would return today, and she wanted to have everything ready by the time he arrived.

Elisabeth pulled a freshly baked loaf of bread out of the oven when she heard a commotion out front. She frowned in concentration as she slowly withdrew the braided loaf, balancing it on the baker's peel. The long handled shovel was heavy and extremely hot as she withdrew it from the oven and she maneuvered it deftly to the small cooking table. With a practiced hand, she dumped the bread onto a cloth she laid out and covered it before replacing the peel in its holder next to the oven. Wiping her hands on her apron, she stepped over to the lamb stew hanging over the fire and stirred it, making sure that the contents on the bottom wouldn't burn before hanging up her apron and moving to the window to see what was going on.

A mule stood tied to the front fence, but since the beasts all looked the same to her, she could not determine who it belonged to. Puzzled, she cautiously walked out the door to see who might be visiting this late in the afternoon. While she could not see anyone, Elisabeth heard noises coming from the side of the house. She rounded the corner and cried out in delighted astonishment when she saw Zacharias and Aaron unsaddling the family animal at the entrance to their small barn. Aaron turned to her with a broad smile, but Zacharias continued to work with the mule as though she were not there. She cleared her throat loudly, hoping to get his attention, but he continued to ignore her.

It wasn't until Aaron put a gentle hand on Zacharias' shoulder and pointed over to Elisabeth that the old man turned and noticed his wife, his eyes lighting up as he focused on her.

Though she was excited to see him, Elisabeth felt the tiniest bit slighted. She placed her hands on her hips and opened her mouth to scold her husband, but before she could get a word out, Aaron spoke up.

"Hold on now, Elisabeth. Before you get too upset, you should know that Zacharias can't hear, so your words would be wasted on him." Her mouth dropped open in horror and shock. Her stricken expression must have alarmed the young priest because he continued, "It will be all right, Elisabeth. From what I understand, it is only temporary. He has been really excited to see you. He even threatened to leave us all behind this morning when he felt that we weren't moving quickly enough to make it back by tonight."

With a chuckle, Aaron paused to stroke the muzzle of the aging animal they were caring for. "As if this old mule could move faster than a canter for more than a league, in any case. There is a lot that we need to tell you, but it would be better if we talked in the house."

Still concerned, Elisabeth calmed upon seeing that Zacharias appeared happy and otherwise healthy. She gave a reluctant nod. As she started toward her husband, a big foolish grin split his wrinkled, bearded face. He dropped the packs he held and rushed to throw his arms around her. A little surprised by Zacharias' public display of affection, she awkwardly patted his back.

He held her for a long time, and after a moment, she relaxed into his warm embrace. Finally, she pulled free and cast a critical eye from the top of his gray head to his sandaled feet. He looked tired, but she had not seen him this excited in a long time.

When he reached down to retrieve the packs, she turned to walk back into the house, still a little embarrassed. With a quick step, Zacharias caught up to her, and still grinning, shifted his load to one shoulder so he could grab her hand. Mortified to hear

Aaron's easy laughter, Elisabeth tried to withdraw her hand. Her husband only linked his fingers in hers and clamped down firmly as they walked through the front door.

"Ooh, that smells wonderful, Elisabeth," Aaron said, stopping as he caught the scent of freshly baked bread.

She turned and smiled at him. "I just pulled it out of the oven. I have some lamb stew that is nearly ready as well." Firmly extracting her fingers from her husband's viselike grip, she pointed at the washroom. "Why don't you and this crazy, old man go and clean off the dirt from your ride while I prepare something for us all to eat?"

As Aaron motioned to Zacharias, trying to get him to understand what she wanted them to do, Elisabeth walked into the kitchen. She quickly pulled the bowls, plates, cups, and eating utensils from a battered chest in the corner and set them out on the low table. She filled a large serving bowl with some of the figs she had purchased on her trip to the market and set out a clay bottle containing freshly pressed grape juice. Before it could slip her mind, she added the honeypot.

As she sprinkled the final seasonings in the lamb stew, Aaron and Zacharias returned. They took their places at the table. Elisabeth brought a pitcher filled with water, a basin, a small cup, and a towel which she draped over a shoulder. She moved first to her husband and dipped the cup into the pitcher. Zacharias held his right hand over the basin and Elisabeth poured the cup of water over it, dipped it back into the pitcher, and poured again. She repeated the process with his left hand, pouring two cups of water over it before handing him the towel so that he could dry off. She then moved to Aaron and repeated the process. When Aaron's hands had been washed, Zacharias stood and washed Elisabeth's hands in the same fashion.

After the ritual cleansing, Elisabeth stepped outside to empty the water into her garden before returning the pitcher, basin, and cup to where they belonged. She set them down and turned toward the stew when the sight of someone standing right behind her made her jump. Zacharias had followed her into the small room unnoticed. While tradition dictated that she serve the men, he had reached for the ladle and was filling the bowls with stew.

Elisabeth started to say something to him, but when he did not look up from his ladling, she just shook her head. Instead, she picked up the bread and a knife and walked back to the dining table. Zacharias set a bowl of stew in front of her and Aaron before returning to stand in front of his own chair. She watched as he opened his mouth to pray for the meal. When no sound came out, he frowned and motioned to Aaron. With a nod, the young man stood and offered the prayer. When he was done, he took his seat and reached for his bowl of stew.

"All right, Aaron, I believe that I have shown admirable patience up to this point. Now would you please tell me what has happened to my husband?" Elisabeth asked.

Aaron nodded, his mouth full of stew, before swallowing and sighing contentedly. "It was the day after we arrived in Jerusalem. Zacharias was chosen through the casting to burn incense in the temple, and—"

"He was? Truly?" Elisabeth burst out.

She faced her husband and watched as Zacharias slathered honey on a thick piece of bread, a smile peeking out from around the corners of his beard.

"Yes. He was very excited about it, but as it turned out, burning incense was only the beginning," Aaron said. "Apparently, while he was in the Holy Place, something miraculous happened. He hasn't shared the details with anyone, but when he came out of the room, he couldn't talk. When I spoke to him, he couldn't hear a word I said. He made a bunch of strange signs to me and the congregation and, eventually, we understood that he'd had a vision, but that he couldn't –or wouldn't– elaborate."

The young priest shrugged. "For the remainder of our service in the temple, he walked around with a silly grin and a dazed expression on his face. We took turns caring for him, but other than his being unable to speak or hear ..." Aaron stopped and looked at Zacharias. "I don't know what to say, Elisabeth. He appears younger than he has in years. He acts as though some great weight has been lifted from his shoulders. I don't understand. I wish he could tell us what he saw in there."

Elisabeth stared in wonder at the familiar face of the man she had loved for so long. *A vision from heaven? How was this possible?* Suddenly she couldn't wait for dinner to be over. As much as she enjoyed Aaron's company under normal circumstances, she wanted him to leave so that she could be alone with her husband. As she gazed at Zacharias, she thought about how she might communicate with a man who was both deaf and mute. The crude signs that he and Aaron had exchanged would not do. As though he could hear her thoughts, Zacharias glanced up. Catching her staring at him, he grinned. Unable to help herself, she smiled back and reached for her forgotten stew.

Elisabeth knew that Aaron was a smart man, and it did not take him long to realize that the couple wanted to be alone. Elisabeth was grateful when he finished the rest of his stew in a hurry and thanked her for the wonderful meal. Pushing her chair back, she joined her husband. Together, they walked the young priest to the door. Gratefully, Elisabeth thanked him for watching over her husband.

"Will you be okay?" Aaron asked smiling at the wrinkled, old man.

"We'll manage," Elisabeth answered. "I will work something out."

Aaron nodded and walked out the door. As he strolled through the front gate he called over his shoulder, "Well, if you need anything at all, you know where I live."

"Many thanks, Aaron," she called with a final wave before turning back to the house.

Elisabeth closed the door and turned to face her husband. He started to move his hands around wildly, but Elisabeth shook her head. She took him by the hand and led him back to the table. She spread some honey on another piece of bread and set it on the plate before him to keep him occupied while she gathered the things she would need. Finding some spare papyrus, a reed pen, and a bottle of ink, Elisabeth set the materials on the low table in front of her husband. She pulled a chair around so that she could sit next to him. Picking up the pen, she wrote *start from the beginning. I want to know everything.*

Zacharias crammed the last bite of bread into his mouth, wiped crumbs from the table in front of him, and reached for the pen. *I have indeed married an intelligent woman. The brethren at the temple let me wave my arms around for days. I think they enjoyed it.* When he caught her gaze, she met his smile with a stern expression. He touched the pen back to the papyrus and wrote about what happened to him at the temple.

She watched, impatience warring with compassion, the tears spilling down his cheeks as he wrote. When Zacharias finally finished, he set down the pen and wiped his eyes with the backs of his hands before passing the papyrus to her. Quickly, she scanned his untidy scrawl. Her eyes widened as she read through what could only be considered a miracle from God. The writing blurred as her vision swam, and she could only stare unseeingly at the papyrus. *I'm going to have a baby.* Feeling Zacharias' comforting arm on her shoulder, she swiped at her eyes with the back of her hand and continued reading.

When she finished, she put down the papyrus slowly and looked at him with hopeful, tear-drenched eyes. To answer the unspoken question, he wrapped his arms around her in a loving embrace. She hugged him back fiercely, not even bothering to wipe her cheek as tears fell anew.

Sobbing with joy on her husband's shoulder, she clung to him. After all this time, she was going to have a baby. The Lord would give her the one thing she had always wanted. Questions of how it was possible never entered her mind, only a silent prayer of thanksgiving for the miracle about to come to pass.

CHAPTER 3

MARY

With a moan, Mary reached up to cover her eyes with a forearm to block out the ray of sunshine. Darkness blissfully returned, and the young girl was tempted to roll over and fall back asleep. Then a single thought wormed its way through her sleep-heavy subconscious. *The betrothal!* Her eyelids fluttered open. *Joseph is bringing the betrothal documents tonight!*

Squealing with delight, she flung back her blankets and leapt up from her mat. She rushed to the window, and pulling back the curtains, stuck her head outside. The cool morning breeze tickled her cheeks. Mary took a moment to simply soak in the morning. Maybe it was her imagination, but everything around her appeared brighter and more vibrant. The sunrise filled the eastern horizon with magnificent hues of burnt orange. Trees and wildflowers burst with life and color.

"Mary!" a voice called from the rear of the house. "Are you awake yet? I have a list of chores that I will need help with before sunset!"

Sighing, Mary pulled her head back inside. Her mother enjoyed making lists. Anna had been making them ever since Mary could remember, and although that usually meant more work to be done, it also made for an organized household. Her mother was nothing if not prepared.

Absently, she ran her fingers through her hair, making a face when they snagged in a handful of snarls. With a second sigh, she picked up her hairbrush and slid a small wooden stool that her father had made for her over to the window. She gazed outside, carefully running the brush through her long brunette hair, wincing occasionally when it caught on a tangle.

"Mary!" Anna called again. "Did you hear me? I said that it is time to—"

"I'm awake!" Mary answered, turning her head to look at the entryway. "I'll be out as soon as I finish brushing my hair!"

"Don't be long, daughter. Your papa has been working since before sunup."

"No, Mama. I won't take long."

Turning back to the window, the young girl nearly fell off of her stool. There, with his arms folded and leaning on the window frame, stood a short, stocky man with brown hair and a bushy brown beard.

"Good morning, Sunshine," he said, smiling so widely that she could see his teeth. "You have a big day ahead of you."

Mary giggled. "Good morning, Papa. Did you sleep well?"

"Well enough, child. Are you nervous?"

Mary tried to shrug nonchalantly but spoiled the effect with a foolish grin. Her father chuckled. Jacob was a well-respected man in Nazareth. People often came from all over the territory to visit their small village just for the opportunity to purchase his leatherwork. On occasion he would allow Mary to visit the shop, and she had seen with her own eyes the wonders her father was capable of creating.

"Of course you are. Who would not be on such a day?" Jacob teased, but then his expression turned serious. "Joseph is a good man, Mary. He is successful and he has an excellent head on his shoulders. I would not agree to this engagement if I didn't trust him."

"I know, Papa," Mary said, feeling the slight hint of a blush on her cheeks. "He has been nothing but kind to me. I am sure he will make a fine husband. I just hope that I will be a good wife for him."

Her father waved that away. "Of course you will, child. Look at the example you have grown up with. As a husband, I could not have asked for a better wife, and now as a father, I could not ask for a finer daughter. You just remember the things your mama has taught you and you will make a wonderful wife."

"But—" Mary protested, her doubts sneaking through.

"But nothing! Do not forget that it was Heli who approached *me*. My cousin wants nothing but the best for his son, and believe me, he has asked for the best."

Mary stood and wrapped her arms around her father's neck. "Thank you, Papa. You always know just what to say."

"I bet if you asked your mama, she'd have a different opinion," he said with a laugh, gently dislodging himself and stepping away from the window. "Now hurry along. You are not the only one in this house who is nervous. If you don't start helping your mama soon, we'll both be in trouble."

Mary's grin was mischievous. "That might be fun to watch."

"Bite your tongue, girl!" he growled playfully. "I've enough on my plate this morning without catching an earful about a certain disobedient daughter. You mind your mama!"

Mary made her eyes as big and innocent as possible. Jacob held his glower for a moment, but then faltered.

"I pity that poor boy," he muttered, turning away from the window. "He has no idea *what* he is getting into."

Mary laughed to herself, thankful that the playful conversation with her father had smoothed out the worst of her nerves. She finished brushing her hair and pulled a suitable robe for housework out of her clothing chest. Once she shrugged into it, she weaved her hair into a braid so that it would be out of the way while she worked.

"I'm ready, Mama!" she called, walking out of her room and into the dining area.

Anna hurried through the front door, pushing back her shawl. She possessed the same thick brown hair and liquid blue eyes as her daughter. She was tall and slender, though her slight build belied a fierce strength of both body and will. "Good morning, daughter. You will find breakfast on the front table. When you finish eating, you'll need this."

Mary groaned when she took a single glance at the heavy wooden rod that her mother held out. The stick was used to beat the dirt and dust out of the interior rug. If there was one job Mary loathed above all others, it was cleaning the rug. The dust and dirt always settled in her hair and clothing, and even worse, it got in her eyes and she would then spend half the day teary-eyed and squinting.

"Mama, can't I—"

"It will do no good to complain, Mary. The rug needs cleaning. Your papa and I have already hung it up outside, where it waits for you."

It is all for me, she reminded herself as she reached out for the rug beater. "Yes, Mama. I'll take care of it."

Anna's eyes widened and Mary was sure that she had prepared herself to answer a sulky child. Mary's submissive obedience must have surprised her.

"Well ... thank you, daughter. Once you finish, let your papa know and he will help you carry it back inside. Mind that you do not let it drag in the dirt. When you are finished with that, you will find the water vessels nearly empty. They need to be refilled."

Mary nodded and stepped over to the table where a bowl full of figs soaked in goat's milk. Pulling out a chair, she leaned the rug beater against it and took a seat. She bowed her head and offered a prayer of thanksgiving before delicately picking out a fig with two slender fingers. As she ate, she thought about the upcoming festivities, and before she knew it, the figs were gone.

She drank from a cup of water to rinse down the meal before wrapping her fingers around the heavy club and shuffling outside. Not far from the house stood two olive trees with a thick rope strung between them. The large rug was draped over the rope. Mary glared at the hateful dirt collector. The patterns on the rug were slightly faded from years of cleanings and foot traffic, but still, it was in good condition. Mary could see crusty dirt clinging to the soft fibers.

Heaving one last sigh, she lifted the heavy, wooden beater to her shoulder and swung. A huge cloud of dust billowed out the moment her stick connected with the large piece of fabric hanging on the line in front of her. Squinting, she turned her face away in an effort to keep the dust from her eyes, but it slid through her half-closed eyelids all the same. Gritting her teeth, she cocked back her arms and swung again.

Over and over she attacked the carpet. As she did, her body fell into the mindless rhythm of it, allowing her thoughts to drift to the evening's upcoming festivities. She was going to be *betrothed!* The giddy, nervous feeling she felt earlier that morning welled inside her again. She could not help grinning. *It is really happening!*

She warned herself not to let her emotions get the best of her, but it was hard to contain them. When the carpet finally quit shedding dirt, she paused, panting in the morning breeze. Stepping out of the dust cloud, Mary dropped the large stick and swung her long braid over her shoulder. She shook her aching hands and massaged her tired arms. More than anything, she wanted to reach up and rub her watering eyes, but she knew that if she did so, it would only make things worse. Instead, she gripped her robes with both hands and jumped up and down, shaking vigorously in an effort to dislodge some of the dirt.

When she was done, she picked up the beater and walked to the other side of the rug. With a scowl, she noticed that this side was filthier than the last. Blowing at a strand of stray hair that fell in front of her eyes, Mary whipped her arms back over one shoulder. She leaned into the swing, satisfied with the loud thwack and the large amounts of dirt that fell away when she connected. *One more side,* she said to herself, and then she could go in and scrub the dirt out of her face and hair.

Settling in, Mary thought back on her first real meeting with the carpenter. Nazareth was not a large city, and Heli, Joseph's father was her second cousin. Even so, she really had not associated much with his son, Joseph. The young man was a few years older than she. He lived on the opposite side of town, nearer the market and his family's carpentry shop. It came as quite the surprise to her when her mother first mentioned that Heli expressed an interest in her as a possible wife for his son. The weight of the rug beater seemed to lessen as memories of their first meeting after discovering the news of their upcoming engagement flooded through her mind.

"The carpenter's shop is just down there, Mary," Ruth said with a giggle, pointing down a side street.

"I know!" Mary said, swatting at her cousin's arm. "I'm nervous enough without you doing that!"

"Aren't you at least a little curious? It isn't like he owns the whole street. He might not even know who you are."

"He's my cousin, Ruth," Mary retorted. "I'm sure he knows. After all, I *am* going to be his wife."

"At least he is handsome. Some of girls end up with men that are four or five times older than them. Joseph is still   young … and strong. Come on, I want to see his shop." Ruth tugged on Mary's sleeve. "Do you suppose he is a good carpenter?"

Mary shrugged. "There are four other carpenter shops in the village, so he would have to be pretty good if he wants to stay in business. Ruth, my father told us to hurry. The cobbler locks his door in less than an hour. Father won't be pleased if we return without his boots."

"All right, all right," Ruth said with a laugh.

Picking up her pace, Mary reached into one of the pockets of her robe, sighing in relief when she felt the tiny metallic coins. It was the first time she would have dealings with the man. She hoped he would not try to take advantage of her because of her youth and inexperience.

Ruth studied the different storefronts. "Which one is it?"

"Father said Ezekiel's was the second shop on the left," Mary answered.

"Girls," a nasally voice called out from one of the vendor carts. "I couldn't help but overhear your conversation, and I must say, your shoes are not in need of repair."

The oily merchant held up a fistful of jewelry. "Why not spend your money here instead?" He pointed a jewel-encrusted finger at Mary. "You would look particularly delightful in pearls, my dear."

"Ooh," Ruth said, taking a couple of steps toward the jewelry vendor. "It wouldn't hurt to look, Mary. Maybe we could try on a few things."

Mary only shook her head. "You can go if you want to, but my father didn't send me here to buy pearls. He needs his boots for work."

"Oh, come on. It won't take long."

Mary had to admit that she was tempted. The pearls on the necklace the man held gleamed in the fading sunlight. He must have sensed her hesitation, because he twisted his hand expertly, and the small white treasures flashed a rainbow of different colors.

"Come now, ladies. Browsing costs you nothing. These pearls come all the way from the coasts of Phoenicia."

Again, Mary shook her head. "I'm very sorry, but I can't. I have business with the cobbler."

With a sympathetic nod, the man turned his attention to Ruth. "And what about you, child? I have a silver studded bar that would look absolutely brilliant tucked into your dark hair."

"I—"

Mary cast a glance over her shoulder and saw that Ezekiel was in the process of taking down his shoe displays. "I can't wait any longer, Ruth. Are you coming?"

Ruth gazed longingly at the jewelry cart before turning away. "I suppose."

Mary hurried to the cobbler's shop. An elderly man paused in the act of retrieving a pair of sandals. "May I help you, young miss?" he asked politely with a bob of his head.

"Yes, please," Mary answered. "My father left a pair of boots with you last week. I am here to pick them up."

"Ah, yes, I have them inside," he replied, ducking into the shop. "They are fine boots. Jacob was quite right to bring them in for repair. They will now last him many more years."

Before she could ask him the price a male voice called out to the cobbler from the street. "Ezekiel! How are you? I have your—Oh, my apologies, I did not mean to disturb negotiations."

Mary turned to look over her shoulder at the man who interrupted them. Joseph was holding the reins of a donkey drawing a small wagon full of wooden furniture. He was taller than most Nazarenes, and his robes stretched taught over broad shoulders and muscular build. His angular face had a sharp nose and a neatly trimmed brown beard. He appeared to be in his late teens or early twenties, but with his youthful face, Mary would not have dared to hazard an exact guess.

"Ooh," Ruth whispered, obviously taken with the handsome man.

Undoubtedly amused with the girls' reaction, Ezekiel smiled broadly and lifted a hand. "Why hello, Joseph! It is no bother at all. I was just concluding my business with these two lovely ladies."

"That's Joseph!" Ruth squealed, digging Mary in the ribs. "Did you hear him? That is Joseph!"

Mortified, Mary cast her eyes to the ground as she felt the blush reach the tips of her ears. A part of her wished the road would open wide and simply swallow her whole. *Why in the world did I bring Ruth today of all days?* Of course it would naturally be that Mary was found in *her* presence when she met the carpenter.

"Do you know Joseph?" Ezekiel asked Ruth quizzically as the young man approached.

"Well, I don't." Mary could hear the edge of laughter in her cousin's voice. "But my cousin does, and I expect she will get to know him even better."

Knowing that Ruth was having too much fun to stop, Mary forced herself to lift her gaze just in time to see the cobbler raising an eyebrow.

"Oh? And why is that?"

"Because they are—"

"I can speak for myself, thank you very much," Mary said, stepping on Ruth's sandaled foot. She masked a smile of satisfaction when Ruth fell silent. Though it was difficult, she stared right into Joseph's deep brown eyes. "Hello, Joseph. It is good to see you again."

The easy smile faded from his face. His color drained. He opened his mouth as if to speak, but no words came out.

"Am I missing something here?" Ezekiel asked, turning from one to the other.

"Um … no," the carpenter managed, still gaping. Then he gave himself a shake and Mary watched as he visibly fought to control his voice. "I'm sorry, Mary. It is good to see you again as well, though it is surprising to find you here."

Mary curtsied, not quite sure what to say next.

"Joseph," Ezekiel demanded, folding his arms, still holding the boots in one hand. "What is going on here? You look as though you've seen a ghost."

The handsome man smiled sheepishly. "My apologies again, Ezekiel. This chance meeting has caught me off guard. As it turns out, my father recently paid a visit to Mary's father and mentioned the prospect of a possible match. He seems to feel that I have spent too much time wrapped up in work, and he is anxious to have me married."

The handsome carpenter turned his attention to Mary. "I probably could have handled this better, Mary, but it isn't every day that a man is blindsided by his future bride. You really are quite beautiful. Do you know that?"

The heat of the blush deepened. Mary wanted to duck her head. "Thank you," she said softly. "It was a pleasure to see you, but I ..."

"Seriously?" Ruth interrupted. "That's it? You aren't even going to introduce me? Fine, I'll introduce myself." She curtsied to Joseph. "I am Ruth, Mary's cousin on her mother's side. So, tell me, carpenter. Do you have a brother?"

"Ruth!" Mary gasped, shocked by the girl's boldness.

Joseph smiled a bit more at ease. "Long since married, I'm afraid. I am the last, and not that far from joining them if my father has anything to say about it," he answered, winking at Mary.

"Well, my congratulations to the pair of you!" Ezekiel's broad grin grew. "I was going to give this young woman the chance to haggle a bit for the boots, but in the light of the upcoming festivities, I believe that we can settle on a price of two denarius."

Mary fingered the coins in her pockets and considered. The cobbler was being overly generous. The price was much lower than she planned to pay. Her father had told her she should expect to pay between four and six of the Roman coins for the cobbler's work. "Are you sure, Master Ezekiel?" She rubbed a denarius between her thumb and forefinger, before counting out the coinage. "That is less than I expected."

Ezekiel's eyes twinkled with assurance. "Young Joseph here has built all of the shelves in my shop, and if I am not mistaken, he is here to deliver the new display table I ordered. He has always treated me fairly. I would not feel right in overpricing his soon-to-be father-in-law."

Mary handed over the amount requested. "That is most considerate of you, Master Cobbler. I am sure that my father will appreciate your generosity."

"I would add my thanks to hers as well, Ezekiel," Joseph said with an appreciative nod. "My purpose was not to put pressure on your negotiations."

The cobbler shrugged Joseph's words away and handed Mary the boots. "May you both live a long life filled with happiness and many children. I'm pleased to have been a part of this meeting. Now, Joseph, about that table…"

Although still dazed at the happenstance meeting of her future husband, Mary remembered her manners. "Thank you, Master Ezekiel."

"Aren't you at least going to bid your future husband farewell?" Ruth asked mischievously. "What must he think of your lack of etiquette?"

Blushing yet again, Mary vowed to fill her cousin's undergarments with mule hair at the very next opportunity. A day full of scratching and dancing around in an attempt to relieve the itchiness would be well-deserved, in her opinion. The girl had absolutely *no* sense of propriety.

"Until next we meet, Joseph," Mary said with a curtsy.

"I look forward to it," Joseph answered, flashing another handsome smile.

"Good day, gentlemen," Ruth said, dropping a curtsy of her own.

The men acknowledged her with a tip of their heads before turning back to their business. Not wanting to give Ruth another chance to embarrass her, Mary grabbed her cousin's arm with her free hand and marched her across the street.

When they were out of earshot, she turned to face the girl. "Why in the name of Moses would you want to humiliate me like that?" she demanded.

Ruth offered a playful wink "He was awfully handsome, wasn't he?"

"Well, yes … of course he was, but that isn't the point."

"Oh, Mary. What would you have done if I hadn't broken the ice? You would probably still be standing there staring at the ground. You should thank me!"

"I'll thank you to mind your own business in the future," Mary muttered, stalking down the street ahead of her cousin. "The man must think me nothing more than a blushing ox."

"Well, if his gaze was any indication," Ruth answered, trotting to catch up, "then he considers you a very pretty ox. He couldn't take his eyes off you."

Suddenly self-conscious, Mary tucked a loose strand of hair behind her ear and walked faster. "You don't know what you are talking about."

"If you will take but a moment to recall, I was not the one who was busy blushing and staring at the ground. I know what I saw. I think Joseph is extremely pleased in his father's selection for a bride."

Well, thought Mary, fighting to keep a silly grin from stealing across her face and ruining the stern position she had just taken with Ruth. *I don't know about Joseph, but if the carpenter is as pleasant and as charming as he appeared this afternoon, I will be* more *than satisfied with the match.*

"Mary! Are you nearly done?"

Mary jumped, and the memory of her meeting with Joseph flitted from her mind as she focused on her mother's voice. "I need you and your papa to put the carpet back in the house so we can set the tables up. There is much to be done before this evening and we are running out of time."

She gave the rug a whack, and felt a twinge of guilt when no dust clouds came out. Now wasn't the time to become lost in daydreams. "I am nearly done, Mama!" She walked around the large carpet once more, giving it small whacks with the beater to make sure that no more dirt fell out.

Satisfied that the rug would pass her mother's inspection, she hurried to the door. "Papa, would you come and help?"

She set the rug beater down with a sigh and stretched her aching arms. Unconsciously, she reached behind her neck and grabbed her long braid of dark hair as she waited for her father to come out. She was just lifting the end of the braid to her mouth when he walked out the door of the house and into the yard.

"You'll hear from your mama if she finds you chewing on your hair again," he teased.

Mary dropped the braid and swung it over her shoulder. "Does she have to know?"

"I think we can let it slide this one time. It is your engagement day, after all." Jacob chuckled, then turned a critical eye to the braided rug. "It looks as if you've done a thorough job on it. To be honest, I'm surprised you didn't beat your way through to the other side. Working out a few nerves, were we?"

Mary nodded sheepishly, thinking it was probably better that her father thought she was just nervous rather than daydreaming about Joseph. He patted her shoulder sympathetically before pushing his way between the two thick sides.

"Are you ready to help me carry it back into the house?"

"Yes, Papa." Mary nodded, reaching out for the two corners behind him.

Together, they worked the large rug off of the line. Her father stood between in the middle, with his hands extended, balancing the carpet on his palms. Mary gripped the ends on each side and curled them in so they wouldn't drag on the dirt. Jointly they shuffled toward the house. After sidling through the door frame, her father tried to align himself with the slight discoloration in the hard-packed, dirt floor where it had lain before. Grunting with the effort, he lowered the heavy fabric while Mary helped him slide it into place, tugging on the corners until it finally lay flat on the freshly swept ground.

"Run and tell Uncle Abraham that I am ready for his help now," her father panted, leaning over to rest his forearms on his knees. "Then you can go in and help your mama with whatever is next on her list while I set everything up out front."

"Yes, Papa." Not wanting to irritate her mother, Mary waited until she was outside before breaking into an excited run for the neighboring house. She slowed when she reached the front door. Knocking forcefully, she rapped her knuckles on the sturdy wooden planks. As she waited, Mary glanced over at the area Abraham and her father had cleared the day before in preparation for the celebration. The door opened, and Mary spun back to see the cherubic face of Abraham's youngest son, Thomas.

"Hello, Mary," he said, smiling up at her. "Are you excited for tonight? I am! Papa says I get to help set up the tables. Do you want me to go and get him? Are you finally ready for us to help?"

Mary grinned at her young cousin. He could talk faster than anyone she knew and he always had so many questions. "Yes, we are ..."

Thomas interrupted her. "I really like Joseph. Did you know that he made my chest? He even carved a horse on the side just because I asked him to! He is really nice, and I bet he's real excited to marry you. Will you live in his shop? What are we eating at the feast?"

"Yes, yes, Thomas," Mary answered, holding up her arms to halt the flood of questions. "He's most kind. I am sure we will live in a house and not his shop. As for the food, well, you will have to wait just like everyone else. Now, would you please tell Uncle Abraham that my father is ready for him to come and help with the tables? Joseph had them delivered last night. If you want to eat anything tonight, I have to go and help my mother prepare it."

"We will be right over," said her uncle as he stepped behind his son and smiled at her. "Thomas, quit pestering the girl. She has a lot going on today. Mary, you can tell my brother that we are on our way."

"Thank you, uncle. I will," Mary said gratefully. She grinned at her cousin, waving as she turned from the door and hurried home to help her mother.

CHAPTER 4

JOSEPH

Feeling a slight sense of urgency, Joseph pushed his broom through the wood chips and sawdust scattered on his shop floor, trying to collect the worst of the mess. A nearly finished yoke sat on his worktable, but it took him longer than expected to carve out the arms to match the measurements he had taken. It still needed to be smoothed and polished, but he would have to finish in the morning. Mary's family expected him any time now, and following the formal declaration of engagement, tradition dictated that he sit through a feast and take the time to meet her family.

Joseph had not meant to work so late, but time escaped him when he lost himself in the complexities of his work. It was one of the dangers of toiling alone in a shop. Under normal circumstances, he enjoyed working late, especially when the alternative meant leaving a task unfinished. Occasionally, his father, Heli, worked with him, but of late he found more and more reasons to stay away. Each excuse sounded plausible, but

Joseph knew the old man was secretly preparing to pass the shop onto him.

At one time, this shop had been a bustle of activity, with Joseph working alongside three older brothers under the careful eye of their father. To Heli's disappointment, Joseph's siblings married and moved away from Nazareth in order to set up their own shops in other parts of Judea. Since his father set the example when Joseph was only a child by packing up his whole family and moving to Nazareth from Bethlehem, Heli wisely kept his disapproval to himself, but Joseph had grown adept at reading the old man. It was part of the reason he resisted the call of the larger markets of Jerusalem and remained to take over the family business. His father's excitement upon learning that his youngest son would take over the shop was worth the occasional pangs of regret that Joseph was letting the coinage of the great cities slip through his fingers.

Today, however, the old man did have a valid excuse. He had been busy meeting with the town scribe in order to draw up the betrothal contract, so Joseph had come in to the shop to finish the yoke on his own. Though his father had lectured Joseph more than once on the necessities of time management, Joseph still struggled with that part of the business. Perhaps having a wife at home would help him with that particular weakness.

With the sweeping finished, Joseph wiped down his tools before returning them where they belonged. He scowled at the unfinished yoke as he removed his apron and hung it up. Another few hours and he would have finished the project. *It can't be helped,* he thought as he checked the latches on all of the windows and the back door.

Gathering his personal affects, Joseph scanned the shop one final time before exiting. He closed the door, pulled out an iron key, and fit it into the lock. The bolt turned easily. He tested the door to make sure that it was secure before slipping the key back into his pocket. Feeling both nervous and excited about the prospect of becoming engaged to such a beautiful and intelligent woman, he hurried down the street toward his house.

Due to his success in carpentry and the skills he gathered through years of experience, Joseph's home was one of the biggest houses on his street. Where many of the dwellings in town were humble, only offering the occupants a single room besides the entryway, his home emulated that of his father's next door.

A large front room for entertaining guests welcomed him. He hoped Mary would appreciate the generous room he set aside for preparing food. The house included two rooms for sleeping on the second level. It also boasted a large roof where he could sleep during the warm summer months and entertain guests when he so chose. As he neared his abode, his mother stood waiting with a basket dangling from one arm. Salome was short and sturdy in build. The top of her head barely reached her son's chest, but she carried the authority of a mother so Joseph always felt as though she looked down on him instead.

He walked up to his door. "Hello, Mama."

"You're running late, my son," she scolded. "You were supposed to be home an hour ago. A fine thing it would be if the groom arrives late for his own betrothal ceremony. What would your father's cousin think of that?"

Knowing his mother, Joseph simply flashed a grin and watched Salome's stern expression melt away. "I am so excited for you, Joseph," she gushed, her stern demeanor melting away. "I can't believe this is finally happening. You certainly kept me waiting long enough."

"Good things are worth waiting for." Joseph bent down and pecked a kiss on her cheek. "So what have you got there?"

She motioned for him to open the door. "Hurry and clean yourself up. I'll show you once we are inside."

Joseph hesitated, a little nervous that she did not come right out and tell him. That was nearly always a bad sign. The need to hurry overrode his suspicions and Joseph opened the door, holding it for the older woman as she bustled inside.

"You are going to need to tidy this up, you know," Salome said, eyeing the interior critically. "This house is in definite need of a woman's touch."

Joseph stepped out the back door to a private area where he could wash the grime from his work off. He only half listened to his mother's steady stream of 'improvements' as he cleaned his hands. His mind continued to reel as he considered his upcoming engagement ... and his future bride. The thought of their chance encounter in front of the cobbler's shop still impressed him. Placed in a difficult situation, the young girl had handled herself most skillfully. He did not know how he would have reacted if their situations been reversed, but Mary possessed the grace and maturity of a much older woman as she worked through the embarrassing moment her cousin had created.

He remembered the instant she had fought through the blush and met his eyes. His breath caught in his chest as if for the first time he witnessed true beauty. She possessed the kind of loveliness that men might fight wars over. Her long dark hair, beautiful blue eyes, lovely full lips, and soft heart-shaped face blended together in as near to perfection as Joseph had ever hoped to see. And yet, he felt the intensity of a fiery, strong-willed woman when she gazed up at him from under those thick lashes. He grinned as he thought about what an excellent wife she would make. Mary had indeed been worth waiting for.

"Joseph! Did you hear me?" Salome called from inside. "I have new robes for you. I've seen what you like to call dress robes, and no son of mine is going to his engagement party in one of those ratty old things. I also bought you some new sandals."

"Thank you, Mother," Joseph answered, suppressing an eye roll.

He knew from years of experience the best way to handle his mother. She had a way of always showing up with things he never asked for. Salome enjoyed surprising her children with gifts and, though they were not always needed, he appreciated the fact that she was always thinking of them. Simple gratitude for her thoughtful gestures was all it took to keep her happy. *Tonight, I definitely want her happy.*

"I'll be right in. If you would, please lay them out on the bed."

Most Nazarenes slept on mats, not having the money to purchase a bed. As a carpenter, Joseph had access to materials and skills that many did not, and he was able to indulge a little when it came to certain comforts and amenities of home life. He wondered what Mary would think about the place once they were officially married and she moved in. He hoped she would be pleased.

Satisfied that he had removed the worst of the sweat and sawdust, Joseph quickly toweled off and slipped into a simple robe he kept outside. He exited the washroom and moved to his bedroom, bracing himself for his mother's surprise. After one glance at his bed, he groaned silently. Joseph's taste in clothing had always been simple and practical, but the elegant robe lying before him was anything but plain.

Where in the world did she find these? He knew it could not have been anywhere in the city. No one in Nazareth had the money or necessity for robes this grandiose. With a sigh, he picked it up and held it to his chest. Knowing that if he said anything it would only hurt her feelings, Joseph slipped it over his head and smoothed it into place. *It's only one night.*

Sitting on the end of the bed, he reached for the new sandals. They were of good make and would serve well enough once he had broken them in. After testing their length against the sole of his foot to make sure they would fit, he laced them on and rose.

"Are you ready yet?" his mother asked, pushing her way into the room. "We have to go. We are going to be ..." Her eyes filled with what he hoped were joyful tears. She blinked as she scrutinized every detail of his new attire. "Oh, Joseph. You are so handsome. You look just like your father did when *we* were married."

Joseph shrugged self-consciously. The robes felt a bit snug in the shoulders and chest to him, but if they made her this happy, he could wear them for the evening. He reached up to readjust the fit, but she slapped his hands away.

"Don't pick at them, Joseph, or they will wrinkle." All business again, she bustled him out of the bedroom and toward the front door. "Now, we really *should* go. Your father has gone on ahead with the betrothal contract."

Joseph gave a glance around the home he would soon share with his new bride one more time before following his mother out the front door. After locking it, he turned to the older woman, reaching to take the basket she held. Still talking faster than he could listen, she linked her arm in his and led him to Mary's house.

His mother continued to chatter as they neared the home, but Joseph, in his nervousness, could not have coherently answered anything she said. When they finally neared the home of Jacob the leather smith, Joseph could hear the scrambling of final preparations. His mother must have heard them too, because she picked up the pace.

"Cutting it a little close, aren't we, Joseph?" Heli called jovially as they walked up to the tables set out for the feast.

"You leave the boy alone, Heli." Salome withdrew her arm and reached out to smooth his robes. "Joseph, you make yourself useful while I go in and help Mary and Anna."

With a nod, Joseph waited for her to step to the open door and disappear inside … without knocking. The woman had no shame. He stood awkwardly for a moment as his father circled around the tables and nudged him in the side with his elbow. "Nice robes."

"This wasn't *my* idea," Joseph muttered as he glared at his father's far more practical attire. "What makes you so special?"

His father laughed and lightly pinched the fine fabric. "Salome gave up trying to dress me years ago, son. You, on the other hand … well, let's just say that sometimes it pays to be the husband instead of the youngest child."

"Don't listen to him, Joseph," Jacob said with a wink. "You look quite handsome. I am sure Mary will be very impressed. Now, all we have left to do is finish setting up the benches and tables. Thank you for your help in procuring them, by the way. Without you, we would have never managed to seat everyone that Anna has invited."

Heli held up the end of the bench he was carrying to emphasize his point. "If you could give us a hand with that, I think we might just be ready in time. The guests should arrive within the hour."

The preparations seemed to pass by all too quickly. Before Joseph realized what was happening, the betrothal tent was erected, the tables were in place, and the guests were arriving. He found himself standing in the large canvas shelter with his father, Jacob, Mary's uncle Abraham, and his father's brother, Stephen. The latter two served as witnesses to the engagement, as demanded by law. Heli sat at a writing table, while Jacob, twirling a pen absently in one hand, chatted with the other men. Joseph paced nervously in front of the table as he listened to the steady murmur of voices coming from outside the tent where the rest of the guests waited.

The noise outside faded until only a hushed silence hung in the evening air. A moment later, pairs of hands reached into the entrance of the tent and pulled the flaps aside to reveal two veiled women. Through his nervous haze, Joseph recognized the stout build of his mother and the thinner, taller frame belonging to Anna. The women entered the tent and held the flaps open as what could only be an angel glided through behind them. It was the only description Joseph's befuddled mind could think as his mouth ran dry.

The young girl was absolutely stunning. Dark curls cascaded down her back, spilling down her elegant white robes. Carefully, she pulled back the intricately laced veil to reveal her face. Joseph didn't know how it could be possible, but whatever had been done to her already lovely features seemed to enhance the beauty tenfold. When she turned the fullness of her gaze upon him, she stole his breath. Her eyes were painted in a way that drew out the deep blue from within. Red dye accentuated the fullness of her lips. Gaping at the stunning vision before him, Joseph felt extremely self-conscious about his own half-hearted preparations.

Mary must have sensed his nervousness, because her lips parted in a quick smile of encouragement. She moved to stand beside him. Anna and Salome took their places, one on each side of the soon-to-be couple. Joseph and Mary turned to face the two patriarchs seated at the writing table.

Joseph's father cleared his throat and picked up the betrothal document. "Now," he said as he studied the couple from his seat. "As you both know, Jacob and I have worked out a bride price and a dowry. These have been written into this contract. However, before it is read and everyone signs it, I would like to speak with each of you about the importance of what is about to happen.

"Marriage is a sacred covenant handed down from the very beginning, ever since father Adam and mother Eve walked the Garden of Eden. From that day, prophets have repeatedly taught us about how important marriage between a man and a woman is to the Lord's plan. God commanded through Moses that 'thou shalt not commit adultery,' and he revealed stern punishments should that commandment be ignored."

Joseph gazed into the face of his future bride as his father continued to talk about the blessings that could come from a successful marriage. Heli explained the purpose of the betrothal period. Joseph was familiar with the custom of waiting before the marriage ceremony, but it was still nice to hear his father's reasoning. Although the promises they made now were essentially wedding vows, Heli taught of the responsibilities each of them were committing to. Heli encouraged Mary more than ever to pay close attention to the way her mother cared for both home and husband as it would not be long before she would forever leave the hearth of her childhood. Her small, perfect features were focused as she concentrated on the words of wisdom, nodding occasionally when she particularly agreed with something that his father said.

"Joseph, you have already come far in preparing for a wife." Heli fixed Joseph with a penetrating stare. "You have a profession and a home, but this is a vital time for your wife. You must exercise patience as she strives to learn the multitude of responsibilities that both wifehood and motherhood present. Do not expect her to know everything immediately. Treat her with respect and understanding. Be good to her. Make sure that both she and your posterity always have a roof overhead and food on the table. Raise your children in righteousness. Be an example to them, and the Lord will bless you in all things.

"I want you to know how happy I am for both of you," Heli concluded. "You are taking the first steps to what is arguably the most satisfying, yet often most difficult, times of your life. If you will love each other and put the feelings of your spouse above your own, you will bring each other more happiness and joy than you can possibly imagine."

As Heli finished talking, Joseph felt Mary slip her small hand into his. He marveled at how soft and delicate it felt in his own calloused grip. Nevertheless, he accepted it and gave it a gentle squeeze.

Jacob cleared his throat and swiped at his eyes with the back of his hand. "Heli, you do this to me every time," he said with a watery chuckle as he rose to his feet. He reached down and picked up the betrothal contract. "I also want to express how happy I am with the decisions you both have made that brought you here. Heli has told you of the joys that marriage can bring, but I want to add that marriage can also bring many trials. Once you settle into this marriage, you will notice that your opinions will differ in many areas."

Jacob's eyes twinkled merrily as he glanced at his wife before shifting his gaze across the table to settle on his daughter. "Mary, when you enter into this marriage, you are giving yourself to Joseph. God commands that when we marry we become one flesh. My daughter, you are covenanting that you will be completely faithful to your husband and that you will be obedient to him. Do not take these vows lightly, for as Heli previously mentioned, the Lord set severe punishments should you break any of these promises. You are marrying a good man and he will provide for you both temporally and spiritually. Know that your mama and I would never have agreed to this marriage if we didn't have faith that he would be an excellent match for you."

Jacob then turned his powerful gaze to his future son-in-law. "Joseph, I strongly suggest that you learn to listen to your wife. Mary is an extraordinary young woman. She is wise beyond her years and her faith is strong. She is kind and hardworking. As you know, many men take it upon themselves to run their households and their wives become little more than property to them. How unfortunate it is for those families. It demeans the women, teaches unfortunate traditions to the children, and oft times the family suffers as a whole due to a lack of unity.

"I urge you to reject this trend. Consult with Mary before making important decisions. She is an intelligent woman, and by heeding her council, you will find that you and your family will benefit from your combined wisdom. As you listen to each other and work through your differences, your respect and love for one another will grow. Your marriage will be strengthened."

Jacob paused to clear his throat again as he studied the scroll. "I will now read the terms of the engagement. If everyone is in agreement, we will then sign the contract and the two of you will be legally betrothed."

Joseph stood, holding his future bride's hand. Her father read through the legal document outlining the bride price that Joseph's family agreed to pay, as well as the dowry that Mary and Joseph would receive from Mary's parents. When he finished, Jacob held a pen out for Joseph to sign. Joseph quickly scrawled his name at the bottom of the parchment and then handed the pen to Mary.

Even her handwriting is lovely, he thought as he watched her neatly write her name below his. She handed the pen back to her father and stepped back to watch as he and the other witnesses signed the document.

Jacob rolled up the scroll and sealed it shut with wax before handing it to Heli. Joseph's father took the document. He tucked it into his robes and grinned at his now betrothed son.

Jacob cleared his throat a third time. "Well, I think we have kept your guests waiting long enough. Let's go out so that they might greet the newly engaged couple." With an extravagant gesture, he motioned them out of the tent.

Joseph grinned foolishly at the roars of congratulations and encouragement filling his ears as he and Mary stepped toward the waiting congregation.

CHAPTER 5

MARY

B right rays of sunlight peaked through Mary's closed curtains. The heat of it burned the back of her eyelids. Balling her hands into fists, she thrust her arms and legs out, stretching from the tips of her fingers down to the ends of her toes. Her big yawn was cut short by a painful wince. Aching muscles protested the stretch and set fire to her limbs. With a sleepy groan, Mary forced herself to sit up.

Pulling her legs out of the blanket, she lazily swung off of her sleeping mat. The stone floor cooled her bare toes as she started to stand. The burning in her legs intensified until she collapsed back on the mat. Ruefully, Mary reached down and rubbed her aching calves. As she massaged, Mary's fuzzy thoughts gradually cleared. Memories of the previous night's activities flickered through her memory.

Images of friends and family, food, singing, and especially dancing peppered her thoughts. No wonder her legs hurt. It was as though her happiness and excitement had lent wings to her feet. She could not remember ever having danced so much in her life! Reaching down, she tenderly felt her toes, wondering if it were possible for her blisters to have formed their own blisters.

The last of the food had barely been eaten before guests pushed back the tables and chairs. Heli and her father built a roaring fire. Musicians began to play. At first, Mary hesitated to join in, content to sit back and watch as Ruth and her other cousins shuffled and stepped in time with the music. Her mother spent a lot of time on her face and hair, so she didn't want to muss it up.

Joseph laughed at her feeble protests, reached down, and plucked her from her seat. She could only grin helplessly at her mother before rushing in with her betrothed to join hands with the other guests around the fire.

The musicians played late into the night. Every time she paused to catch her breath and head for refreshments, someone else would call her back into the circle. After only a few dances, she followed Ruth's lead and removed her sandals. It seemed a brilliant idea at the time. *But now,* Mary thought, reaching down to run her fingertips over her throbbing toes, *perhaps not.*

Even the pain in her legs and feet couldn't keep the satisfied grin from lifting the corners of her mouth. It had been so much fun to be the center of attention. Ruth had been right! All through the night, Joseph seemed unable to take his eyes off of her.

Her smile widened as she recalled the stunned expression on his face when she walked into the tent. Though Mary had often been told that she was pleasant to look upon, nothing made her feel more beautiful than Joseph's open admiration.

Carefully, she shifted her weight to her legs. Knowing what to expect, the pain was not so bad. She glanced into the small bronze mirror hanging over her dresser and could not help but laugh at her bedraggled reflection. Her face was a mess of smudges from the paint her mother expertly applied the day before. Her hair was ratted and disheveled, and large shadows circled under her eyes. That, more than anything else, testified to the amount of fun she had experienced the previous night.

"Well, look who finally decided to join us," her father called from the table when she strolled into the dining room. "My goodness, child! Whatever happened to the fancy girl who walked into the betrothal tent last night?"

"Papa, I am an engaged woman now," Mary scolded, trying her best to appear stern but knowing she failed miserably.

"Ah," Jacob intoned, drawing out the sound. "Someone is getting a little too big for her curls, I see. Sign one official document, and suddenly you are a *woman* and no longer my little girl. Well, if you are all grown up now, then it would be wrong of me to say that you look a frightful mess this morning." He winked at her. "So I won't say it."

Her mother clucked her tongue in mock disapproval. "Well, it is no wonder! She was quite ... exuberant during the festivities." Anna smiled and motioned for Mary to join her out back to help prepare the meal. "I really liked Heli's comments about marriage," Anna said, popping a dried fig into her mouth. She cut into a fresh loaf of bread.

"Yes," agreed Jacob. "He obviously put a lot of thought into them. I've always enjoyed Heli's teachings. He is a wise man."

"I liked how he said that nothing would bring me greater happiness or joy than putting Joseph's feelings above my own," said Mary, stacking the sliced bread onto a platter. "I think Joseph liked that, too."

"He is a good man," replied her father. "So, now that you have met his family, how will you get along with your new in-laws? I gather that you like Joseph and his parents well enough, but what about his siblings and their families? As an only child, you are marrying into a rather large family."

Mary shrugged, practically skipping to where her father sat at the table and set the plate of bread on the table. "They were all really nice to me, but since they don't live here in Nazareth, I expect that I won't see them much. Joseph said that his brothers have wood shops much closer to Jerusalem. The work there keeps them busy so they can't visit much. A couple of his nieces and nephews are close to my age, but last night was the first time that I met most of them. Joseph told me that his father was a little sad when they decided to start their own business instead of work with him, but he was very supportive of their decision."

Breakfast passed pleasantly, with the family discussing the events of the previous evening around bites of bread and honey. *This is nice,* Mary thought, watching as her mother teased her father about his inability to keep time during the dances. Her father in turn poked fun at the fact that her mother had been taller than most of the men. As she watched her parents, Mary began to notice things she overlooked before. She enjoyed how her father managed to compliment his wife even as he teased her, and the casual intimacy her mother displayed when she reached out and rested her hand on Jacob's forearm. *I hope one day Joseph and I develop a similar relationship.*

Anna rose from the table. "We have a lot to do today. Feasts are fun, but they do require a lot of work both before and after."

"I talked with Abraham last night," her father added. "He has agreed to help me finish cleaning up outside. When we finish, we will rebuild the fence between our houses."

Her mother nodded. "I have many things that need to be returned to their rightful owners. Jacob, before you start working out in front, will you hitch the cart to the mule?"

With an exaggerated sigh, Jacob nodded and turned to Mary. "There has always been something about a peaceful, quiet morning that irritates your mama for some reason."

"Mary," Anna continued, making a point to ignore Jacob. "Clear the table and watch for the cart. When it arrives, I will need your help to load it. Following that, I'm leaving you in charge of the house. You know what needs to be done." She winked at Jacob. "We need to get all of the help out of her that we can. We don't have much more time remaining until it will be just you and me."

Her father grinned at Mary and pushed his chair back from the table. "I think we'll be fine. If you haven't noticed, Mary is the cause of most of these big messes anyway."

"We'll see about that," Mary answered sweetly, catching her parents' rhythm. "Soon enough, you'll be begging me to come back."

All of them laughed. Jacob gave Mary's shoulder a squeeze before walking out the door toward the small stable.

"Mary," her mother said when it was just the two of them. "Why don't you change out of your nightclothes, wash your face, and brush your hair so we can start loading that cart as soon as your papa is ready. I'll clear the table."

"Thank you, Mama," Mary answered, grateful her mother gave her a little time to pull herself together. As she walked past the slender woman, she leaned in and gave her a big hug. "Thank you for making last night so special for me. I love you both so much."

"Of course," her mother said, patting her on the back. "We love you too, child. Now hurry along. We are already off to a late start."

Mary dressed quickly, but by the time she was done, her mother had already begun to fill the cart with the bundles that she would be returning to her neighbors. Mary rushed to help. Working together, it did not take long for them to prepare the first load.

When everything was secured, Mary bid goodbye to her mother and turned to study the house. *Now where do I start first?* she pondered, scanning the rooms. She wanted to have everything completed by the time her parents returned, as a way to thank them for all of their hard work the previous night. *Maybe if I finish early, I'll have the chance to sneak down and see Joseph before he closes up.*

The possibility of a visit to Joseph's wood shop motivated her to work quickly, but even so, the cleaning took longer than she hoped it would. *Still,* she thought glancing up at the sun, noting that it had already marched three-fourths of the way through its celestial route, *I should have enough time, and we are betrothed after all.* Slightly giddy with excitement, she hurried to rinse her face and change her robes once again. She wanted Joseph to see her in something a little more … appropriate.

On her way out of the house, she filled a clay pitcher with water and set it on a tray next to two cups. With careful balance, she carried the tray out to her father and Uncle Abraham.

"You are a blessing, child," Abraham said, smiling as she approached. "Hold on now, Jacob. I need a drink."

Expertly balancing the tray on one hand, Mary waited for her father to set down the large piece of wood he cradled in his arms. She passed one cup to her uncle and handed the other to her father.

"I'll just leave the tray out here, Papa." She lifted the pitcher to fill their cups. "I've finished everything Mama wanted me to do. If it is okay with you, I'd like to go and see Joseph."

"Daughter…" Jacob took a couple of greedy gulps from his cup, wiped his lips with the back of his hand, and made his tone stern. The twinkle in his eye stayed. "You know better than that. The future bride is to have no contact with the husband until after the wedding."

"Of course, Papa," Mary said slyly. "Mama told me how strict you were to that particular tradition during the time of your engagement."

Uncle Abraham chuckled. "She has you there, Jacob. I seem to recall multiple times that you had 'business in the city.'"

Her father gave a jovial laugh. "So I did, so I did. I am sure that Joseph will be thrilled with your visit. Just be sure to observe the proprieties of the situation. Thank you for all of your help today, and for the water."

Mary smiled gratefully at him. "Don't let Uncle Abraham drink it all," she teased as she walked toward the street, "and tell Mama that I will be back in time to help with dinner."

Excitement lightened Mary's step as she approached Joseph's shop. It was midafternoon by the time she made her way to town, but she felt sure her future husband would still be at his wood shop. Ever the diligent worker, Mary reasoned Joseph would be trying hard to catch up. The betrothal must have put him behind. Idly, she wondered if things would be different between them now that they were engaged. She had heard tales of husbands who grew nervous after the betrothal and put up a barrier between them and their future wives.

Mary did not have long to worry. Joseph burst through the open doorway of his shop as she crossed the street. Running to her, he wrapped her in a giant hug, lifting her off the ground. Although she had not expected the sudden outpouring of public affection, it pleased her immensely. Joseph must have missed her as much as she missed him.

"Mary! I'm so glad you came. There are so many things I want to discuss with you. Do you have time to stay? I have nearly finished my work and I would love to escort you home."

Mary nodded eagerly. "I have finished my tasks, and Father has granted me permission."

Taking her hand in a firm grip, he led her into the shop. Once inside, he propped the door open with a piece of wood and slid an ornate chair in front of the door.

"To keep any passersby from becoming too suspicious." He offered her a roguish wink. "You know how people love to talk."

"Perhaps I should not have come." Mary cast a fretful glance over her shoulder. "I would hate for people to get the wrong idea."

"Nonsense. Simply keep yourself within full view of the street. There is much I would like to discuss with you."

Mary pointed curiously at a large piece of wood. "Who is the yoke for?"

"It will belong to Hezekiah, the olive merchant … as soon as he makes the final payment."

Mary giggled. "I've heard stories about him. Have you had trouble with him in the past?"

"Not personally, no." Joseph raised an eyebrow. "I have, however, been warned of his … reluctance to pay. Once a buyer has been accused of such, a prudent businessman demands to see the money before delivering the goods."

"So what are you doing to it now?"

He held out an oil-stained rag. "One of the secrets to my success here in Nazareth is that I give all my creations three extra coats of polish beyond what is required. It takes a bit longer and is more expensive, but the end result is a higher quality product. I want nothing but my best work to pass through these doors."

He began polishing the large shaft of curved wood. The sureness of his movements impressed Mary. When Joseph glanced up from his project and caught her staring, she felt the beginnings of a blush on the back of her neck. Graciously, as though sensing her embarrassment, he returned his focus to the yoke.

"Enough about my work. I want to know what you thought of last night."

"Oh!" Mary scooted forward on her chair in excitement. Absently reaching behind her, Mary caught the end of her braid and started to lift it to her mouth. As soon as she realized her intentions, she dropped it over her shoulder. "Wasn't it lovely? Your father's advice was most impressive."

Joseph nodded. "Papa has always had a way with words."

"It made me a little nervous, all that talk about responsibility and being a good wife and mother. There is a lot I still don't know."

"A lot we both still don't know," Joseph said gently. "That is the joy of marriage, Mary. We will figure it all out together. I am excited to start my life with you. I am sure we will both make mistakes, but I promise to be patient with you if you will do the same for me."

Grateful tears welled. Joseph's kind words eased her troubled mind. "How is it that you know exactly what I need to hear?"

"A future husband's intuition?" The lift at the end of Joseph's question made her chuckle.

"That must be it." She gave a teasing nod. Her confidence faltered. She forced herself to ask, "So what did you think of the evening?"

"I think …" He paused, circling to the other side of the yoke. "I think that my future wife is an enthusiastic dancer."

"Joseph!" Mary's voice raised in protest. "That's not what I mean."

"What?" His eyes widened in mock innocence. "It is the truth. I don't think anyone out there could keep up with you."

"Hmmm." Mary sat back in her chair, measuring the sincerity of his words against the twinkle in his eye. His mischievous grin pleased her. "Maybe that is so. Did the ceremony leave any other impressions on you?"

Talk of their future life together made the evening pass in a quick and pleasant manner. Before Mary realized it, Joseph was closing the shop and escorting her home. Their conversations of the future still made her feel slightly giddy. It was actually going to happen! In one year, she would leave her parents and start her life together with Joseph.

As the last red-orange fingers of sunlight withdrew, Mary sat on her familiar stool running a comb through her hair. She loved ending the day like this. A single candle on her windowsill danced in the cool night breeze. The repetitive motion allowed her mind to engage in other matters. Considering all that transpired over the last couple of days, she had a lot to ponder.

Wincing as she worked her comb through a particularly stubborn tangle, Mary noticed the room was brighter than it should be for this time in the evening. She glanced at the candle in front of her, but it gave off the same dull, flickering light it always had. Confused, Mary set down her comb and turned slowly on her stool. The strange source of light emanated from the middle of the room. She stared incredulously as it intensified until the brightness forced her to shield her eyes. Power radiated from the midst of the glow, paralyzing her with its intensity. She sat frozen in wonder as, for the first time in her life, the brilliance of God's might filled her. Never before had Mary expected to feel such a combination of love, security, hope, and authority that now filled her being. She did not know how she could stand it, and all at once her own imperfections seemed to magnify exponentially.

Within the midst of the dazzling light, a voice spoke. "Hail, thou that art highly favoured, the Lord is with thee: blessed art thou among women."

Trembling at her own unworthiness, Mary squinted into the brilliance. The light faded until it outlined a figure robed in white. It appeared to be a man, but nobody could radiate the power and majesty that Mary felt as she gazed upon this heavenly being. The angel's manner of speech was formal, and Mary could not quite grasp his meaning. *Highly favoured? The Lord is with me? Blessed among women? Could he be talking about my engagement with Joseph?* He must have sensed her confusion because he smiled kindly, his bright blue eyes twinkling in merriment.

"Fear not, Mary: for thou hast found favour with God."

Mary calmed at his reassuring words, but the next thing that the messenger said sent her mind reeling.

"And, behold, thou shalt conceive in thy womb, and bring forth a son, and shalt call his name JESUS. He shall be great, and shall be called the Son of the Highest: and the Lord God shall give unto him the throne of his father David: and he shall reign over the house of Jacob for ever; and of his kingdom there shall be no end."

Mary slid off the chair, her legs folding under her as she listened in awe to the angel's words. She *knew* of this prophesy. It was said that one day a Messiah would be sent from Heaven to rescue the Jews. *Wait, did he say that I would be the mother of this Jesus?*

How can I possibly be the mother of a king? It took several moments more before the realization struck her and she reached a shaking hand to her heart. *How can I possibly be worthy enough to raise the literal Son of God?*

Even as the questions formed, a wonderful peace descended upon her and reassured her troubled mind. As fantastic as the messenger's words sounded, if this was the will of God, then there was no question of compliance. As the feelings of comfort calmed her moment of worry, another question occurred to her. She was betrothed, but she would not be married for quite some time. How would this miracle be physically possible? She studied the messenger's face. The kindly angel gave a gentle nod as though encouraging her to voice the unspoken question.

"How shall this be, seeing that I know not a man?" she asked, matching the angel's formality with her own.

"The Holy Ghost shall come upon thee, and the power of the Highest shall overshadow thee: therefore also that holy thing which shall be born of thee shall be called the Son of God."

Mary lowered her head as understanding of the angel's words filled her. She wished she had someone else there to talk to, someone who might understand the full import of the angel's tidings. She knew her parents would listen and believe, but she was not sure they would fully understand. How could she possibly explain in words the way she felt at this? Could anyone comprehend her emotions at the prospect of a heavenly visit? She wanted to leap in the air in an effort to vent the excitement coursing through her. At the same time, it was all she could do to keep from weeping openly with the sheer joy of it.

Again, as though understanding the questions in Mary's heart, the messenger answered her silent inquiry. "And, behold, thy cousin Elisabeth, she hath also conceived a son in her old age:

and this is the sixth month with her, who was called barren. For with God nothing shall be impossible."

Full of gratitude that this holy personage had once again set her mind and heart at ease, Mary nodded, a steady resolve way beyond her tender years building within her. She met the angel's expectant gaze. "Behold the handmaid of the Lord: be it unto me according to thy word."

The messenger's reassuring smile strengthened her determination to give herself fully to the Lord. The light surrounding him intensified. Mary held his eyes for as long as she could, but it grew to such a dazzling brightness that she was forced to turn away. When she could again see, the heavenly visitor had vanished. The room looked as it always had. Only the light from the lamp remained, casting flickering shadows off the surrounding walls.

For a long time, Mary knelt on the cold, stone floor of her room as she pondered the angel's words. The messenger had gone, but the peace and comfort he radiated remained. *I am to be the mother of the Son of God.* As unbelievable as it sounded, *she* had been chosen to raise the Messiah. Unadulterated truth flooded through Mary, leaving no room for doubt. In an instant, hope and belief were replaced with pure knowledge and total understanding. Slowly, Mary pushed herself to her feet. Exhaustion overtook her—both mentally and physically. It was as though the heavenly visitation sapped away every bit of her strength.

On trembling legs, she managed to stumble to her sleeping mat before collapsing on it. Her body begged for sleep, but Mary's mind refused to disengage. For hours, the holy visitation played over and over in her head. Long after the candle burned out the memory slowed, inviting her mind to rest. She curled into a comfortable sleeping position. An image of Joseph's kind face invited her to join him in peaceful slumber. She returned her betrothed's welcoming smile, eager to share her wonderful news.

As Mary searched for the perfect words to relay the miraculous visitation, a terrible realization exploded in her mind. Peace shattered like a priceless vase dropped from careless fingers. Alarm shuddered through her body, thrusting her into a sitting position, popping her eyes open in horror. Panic mounting, her lungs refused to fill with air. She clutched at her chest, willing herself to breathe.

The most devastating and powerful question she had ever thought echoed through her head. Over and over the words pounded like a carpenter's hammer on a stubborn nail: *How will I ever tell Joseph?*

The following morning, Mary sat at the breakfast table and stared at the food set out in front of her. The events from the previous night continued to run through her mind.

"Mary, are you well?" asked Anna, her voice heavy with concern. "You haven't eaten anything. Are you feeling ill?"

Roused from her contemplations, Mary looked at her mother, blinking to focus her thoughts. How could she even *begin* to describe what she was feeling? Last night, an angel told her that she was to be the mother of the Son of God. How could she possibly explain what had happened?

"What's wrong, Mary?" Jacob asked.

Hearing the worry in her father's tone, Mary opened her mouth to speak, but no words came out. Anna reached out a hand and rested it on her forehead.

"Well, she doesn't feel warm Jacob, but maybe she should go and lie down, just in case."

"I'm fine, Mama," Mary said hoarsely. "It's just that something … happened last night."

"What do you mean happened? Does it have to do with Joseph? Is he okay? Did you two have a fight? You seemed so happy when he walked you home."

"No, Mama, Joseph and I are fine."

Anna opened her mouth to say something else, but Jacob held up a hand to quiet her.

"Go ahead, Mary," he said reassuringly.

Mary took a nervous breath. " I am with child."

Both of her parents gasped in surprise. Her father blinked in confusion, his fist tightening on the table. Mary waited for him to speak as he struggled for control, but said nothing.

Her mother recovered first. "How do you know? Tell us what has happened, child." She spoke carefully, as though hoping she had misheard.

Hesitantly, Mary began to describe the miraculous visitation. As she spoke, she glanced at her parents. She expected the stunned amazement she saw on her mother's face, but her father's reaction surprised her. He was gazing at her with rapt attention, his eyes wet as he hung on her every word.

"Mary," he whispered when she concluded, "this is wonderful." He reached up and wiped tears away from his rough cheeks with the backs of his hand. "I can't believe this is really happening." Leaping to his feet, he hurried around the table and wrapped his arms around his daughter.

"Thank you, Papa," Mary sobbed, clinging to him as he held her. "It's … just that I don't know what I am going to tell Jo—" She started to speak, but her father cut her off.

"Don't worry about that now." Her father knelt down in front of her and looked her in the eye. "Mary, I don't know if you understand exactly how exciting this news is. Prophets have foretold of this event from the very beginning. Even I don't understand the full import of this, but I do know one thing. There is absolutely no reason for you to feel ashamed or afraid. This is glorious news, my child! The Savior of the world is finally going to come to earth. He is going to save us all, and you are to be his mother!"

With a huge grin, he hugged her again and turned to her mother. "I suppose that would make us his grandparents. That's a little intimidating when you really think about it. And the angel said Elisabeth is is with child as well? I wish I could have been there when Zacharias received *that* news!"

Mary's mother rose with a quiet grace and put a hand on Mary's shoulder. "I'm so happy for you, my daughter. You have lived a worthy life indeed if you are to be entrusted with this. I know that I speak for your papa as well when I say that we are honored to be your parents. Would you like to go see Elisabeth?"

"Oh, yes, Mama!" Mary bubbled anxiously. "There *must* be a reason the angel told me that she was with child. I would very much like to see her." She couldn't believe how fortunate she was. What parents but hers could be presented with such news from a young girl and accept it at face value?

"Well, that settles it," Jacob said, rising to his feet as well. "You and your mama pack everything we shall need. I will close up the house and the shop. As soon as I am finished, I'll hitch the mule to the cart. It has been quite some time since our last visit to Hebron. I suppose a little time in the countryside will do us good."

"Papa," Mary protested. "Are you sure you can leave the shop right now? What about all of your customers? It will take at least three days to make the journey."

"You let me worry about that. Hurry along, child. We have much to do before we depart."

Mary rose, and since her parents were both standing so close together, she wrapped her arms around both of them. "Thank you for believing me," she whispered.

"You have never been anything less than honest with us, my girl," her father reassured, patting her hair. "Of course we believe you."

Mary nodded, fighting back the fresh batch of tears that threatened to spill over her already damp cheeks. She reached down and picked up the dishes, preparing to clear the table.

"No, Mary," her mother said, taking the items out of her hands. "I will take care of this. You should go and see Joseph. He should know where we are going."

Mary froze at the mention of her betrothed's name, feeling the color drain from her face.

"You don't have to tell him about the angel now, child. Just let him know that we will be going to Hebron for a few days," Anna said, correctly reading Mary's panic. "There will be time enough to break the rest of the news to him upon our return."

"Yes, Mama."

Trying to calm her jumbled nerves, Mary smoothed her dress and stepped away from her parents and toward the front door. She felt a pang of sadness at the thought of leaving Joseph behind, but the prospect of a visit to Hebron excited her. Her cousin, who had been considered barren for more years than Mary had been alive, was expecting! Surely Elisabeth would understand better than *anyone* what Mary was about to experience.

Anxious to be on her way, Mary picked up her pace, hurrying toward the shop of the carpenter she would one day marry.

Uncertain as to how she would explain the angelic visitation when she returned from Hebron, Mary felt certain of one thing. She felt sure that Joseph would believe her.

CHAPTER 6

ELISABETH

Elisabeth glanced up from the table at the sound of a timid knocking sound coming from the front of the house. Craning her neck, she peered through the window next to the door, but from where she was seated, Elisabeth could not see the visitor.

"Zacharias!" she called from where she sat kneading the dough. "Someone is knocking! Could you answer the door?"

When she heard no answer, she sighed and wiped her flour-coated hands on her apron. With a groan, she carefully pushed herself to her feet.

Of course he could not hear the door … or her … or anything at all. Slowly, she worked her way around the table, putting a hand on her throbbing back as she moved. She knew that her husband's current condition was the result of a perfectly natural response to the news given by Gabriel in the temple. There were times, however, that she wished the old man could have simply kept his questions to himself.

Moving around the house was becoming increasingly difficult. *There is a reason that having a baby was meant for young women and not the elderly,* she thought, taking deep breaths as she waddled into the small room they used to receive guests. Though she counted her blessings every day that her womb had been opened, pregnancy was not easy. She took so many aspects of her youth and vitality for granted as a young girl. Now, her back hurt all of the time, her feet were nearly always swollen, and the joints in her knees began to ache if she were on her feet for more than a couple of minutes. If she ached this much at six months, she could not imagine how she would feel when the time came to deliver.

Stop complaining, she ordered herself, pausing near a chair in the front room so she could rest for a moment. *This is what you have always wanted.* To be fair, her husband tried his best to make sure that she was comfortable. He offered to bring in someone to help with the cooking and cleaning, but Elisabeth made it clear to him that she would continue with her normal duties. As soon as he understood, he bought a tall sturdy stool that she could use for food preparation, in order for her to avoid having to stand for extended periods of time. He also worked harder around the house in order to make things easier for her. If she were slated to carry a child this late in life, at least she had the good fortune to be married to a man such as Zacharias.

Her only major complaint was that he was no longer equipped to handle the unexpected, small things, like answering the door, for example. The knock sounded again, and Elisabeth huffed out a large breath, pushing away from the chair.

"I am coming!" she called. "One moment!"

She reached the front door and lifted her hand to pull the door open when she felt the baby kick. With a smile, she reached down and gently touched her protruding belly. For a moment, she stood there, enjoying the intimate connection that only a mother and child can truly understand.

Swinging open the door, Elisabeth hesitated, studying the beautiful young woman standing in front of her. Recognition struck her and Elisabeth gasped with pure delight. "Oh, Mary! My, what a wonderful surprise! You have grown so much since our last meeting."

"Hello, Elisabeth," the young girl answered with a shy smile. "How are you?"

Elisabeth swung the door open wider and peered out. "Are you alone, child? What could have possessed your father to allow you to travel all this way on your own?"

"Oh, no. My parents stopped at the market. They wanted to pick up a few things before arriving. They told me I was welcome to come ahead. I hope that is all right."

"But of course! It has been quite some time. Won't you please come in?"

Mary bowed her head in gratitude. "Thank you, cousin." She followed Elisabeth through the door. "I have been very excited to see you. There is much I would like to discuss with—"

"Oh!" Elisabeth winced, grabbing her stomach with both hands. Her belly lurched.

It was not a kick. She had experienced kicks before, and they felt nothing like this. It was almost as though the baby thrust out with both legs. Turning slowly, she stared at the young girl behind her with wide brown eyes. As she continued to hold a hand to her abdomen, she sensed a familiar warmth as the Holy Ghost fill her. In that instant Elisabeth saw everything clearly. The spirit testified the truthfulness of her observations. She understood the reason for her child's unexpected surge of excitement.

Her cousin was *not* standing alone as she had originally thought. This young girl was also carrying a child, one that would have an even more profound impact on the world than her own.

"Blessed art thou among women," she intoned, the formal mode of speech she saved for prayer coming to her lips unbidden. "And blessed is the fruit of thy womb. And whence is this to me, that the mother of my Lord should come to me?"

Reaching out, she took hold of Mary's shoulders. The fire inside threatened to burst forth. When she saw the startled expression on the young girl's face, she continued.

"For, lo, as soon as the voice of thy salutation sounded in mine ears, the babe leaped in my womb for joy."

Elisabeth grinned when Mary's eyes filled with tears. The young girl smiled and stepped closer, wrapping her arms around her.

"My soul doth magnify the Lord," Mary answered in kind. "And my spirit hath rejoiced in God my Saviour. For he hath regarded the low estate of his handmaiden: for, behold, from henceforth all generations shall call me blessed. For He that is mighty hath done to me great things; and holy is his name. And his mercy is on them that fear him from generation to generation.

"He hath shewed strength with his arm he hath scattered the proud in the imagination of their hearts. He hath put down the mighty from their seats, and exalted them of low degree. He hath filled the hungry with good things; and the rich he hath sent empty away. He hath holpen his servant Israel, in remembrance of his mercy; as he spake to our fathers, to Abraham, and to his seed for ever."

Elisabeth pulled back slightly, gazing in awe into the face of this chosen vessel. Her own eyes filled with tears as she soaked in Mary's sweet testimony. "The Lord has indeed chosen well," she whispered, letting go of the formality and drawing Mary back to her. "You will be well-suited to the task of raising the Savior of mankind."

At that moment, Mary's parents tapped on the open front door. Elisabeth dropped her arms and stepped away from her young cousin.

"Good evening, Elisabeth!" Jacob said with a knowing smile. "I see that Mary has already revealed her news, though I must say that I am slightly disappointed. I had hoped that she might wait until we arrived."

"I didn't have to, Papa!" Mary said with a relieved chuckle. "Elisabeth knew as soon as she answered the door!"

"I am sure she was exaggerating, if she told you that," Anna said, with a tiny grin. "Though, to be honest, I would have expected this kind of jest more from Zacharias. Perhaps pregnancy has changed Elisabeth more than we think."

"The spirit reveals many things," Elisabeth said, casting Mary a private, knowing smile. "Well, come in, both of you! Don't simply stand there with the door open. I was just preparing supper. My husband and I would love it if you joined us."

"We apologize for dropping in on you unexpectedly," Mary's mother said, stepping forward to grasp Elisabeth's outstretched hands. "But when we learned of your ... condition, we felt it would be in Mary's best interest to spend a little time with you. We picked up a few things to try and lighten the burden. It won't take but a moment for Jacob to unload the cart."

"There is no need of that," Elisabeth chided. "We are family. You are always welcome here. However, the food will be much appreciated. Jacob, come in and greet Zacharias before unloading the cart, as I am sure he will want to assist. However, there are a few things we should discuss before I take you in to see him."

"Is he all right?" Anna's mouth dropped open with concern. "He's not sick, is he?"

"Oh, no." Elisabeth flapped her hand impatiently. "Nothing like that ... well, not *exactly* like that. He ... ran into a little trouble at the temple a little while ago."

Mary arched a knowing brow. "Does it have anything to do with the pregnancy?"

"As a matter of fact, it does." Knowing that her answer was hardly satisfactory, Elisabeth puffed out a breath through pursed lips. "I suppose that I had better explain things before you greet him. Otherwise it could take us all night."

She motioned to the open bench in the front room and crumpled into the chair nearest to her. With a sigh of relief, she folded her arms on her lap as she waited for her guests to seat themselves in the remaining chairs.

"About six months ago, Zacharias returned home from the temple with some fairly unbelievable news," she started once everyone was seated. "On the first day of his temple assignment period, he was chosen to burn incense. While in the Holy Place, he was visited by an angel."

As she told the story, Elisabeth noted that Mary and her family seemed surprised at Zacharias' becoming deaf and mute, but the idea of an angel descending from heaven bearing strange tidings did not cause them to flinch. Casting a quick glance at her young cousin, inspiration hit Elisabeth. *Mary must have her own story to tell.*

"He can't hear or speak?" Jacob asked, his voice incredulous.

"Believe me, it has been more difficult for me than it has been for him," Elisabeth said with a weary smile. "Much of the time, he sits around with his nose buried in the writings of the prophets."

When she caught the disapproving look on Anna's face, she shook her head and made her smile more pleasant. "No, cousin. He is eager enough to help whenever I ask anything of him, but most often it is simply easier to do things myself rather than track him down and write down exactly what I need. Cheaper, too," she added. "We have been going through mounds of parchment as it is."

"But, why was he cursed?" asked Mary. "Was it simply because he questioned the angel? If this visitor is the same as the being that visited me, why was I not similarly stricken? I also questioned the messenger, but he just smiled at me and answered."

Elisabeth smiled reassuringly at her cousin. "Why don't you tell me about what happened to you? Then I will try to answer your question."

"Yes, cousin," Mary said with a nod. "It happened a few nights ago. The night after my engagement to Jos—"

"You are engaged?" Elisabeth exclaimed. "Why, congratulations child! That is wonderful! How long—"

Seeing a flash of pain fill Mary's eyes, Elisabeth stopped short in her celebratory words. "My apologies for the interruption, Mary. Please continue."

"Well." Mary paused to clear her throat. "I was preparing for bed, and this light filled my room. At first I couldn't even see into the center of it, because it was so bright. Before it could burn my eyes, it dimmed until I could see a man standing in the midst of it. He told me that I was favored of the Lord and called me by name."

Although Mary's eyes lifted upward, Elisabeth knew her cousin did not see the ceiling.

"He told me that I would bear a son, and that his name would be Jesus. He said that Jesus would be ... the Son of God."

Mary paused and wiped tears from her eyelashes.

Elisabeth's joy swelled as she listened in amazement. She ached to wrap her arms around her cousin. Acting on the impulse, she reached over and hugged the young woman. This was all so amazing. What Mary said confirmed what her own husband had told her about their child, John. Now she knew what Zacharias had meant when he said that the baby would be filled with the Holy Ghost right from the womb. John had known that Mary carried his cousin, who was also the Son of God. That must have been the reason for his bout of frenzied excitement.

Mary didn't speak.

"So what did you ask the angel?" Elisabeth urged. To her surprise, the young woman blushed prettily, casting a quick glance up to her father. "It is all right, Mary," Elisabeth assured her, not wanting to further embarrass the girl. "There is no need to answer if you'd rather not."

Mary shook her head, staring down at her sandals. "I ... asked him how it was possible for me to have a baby, since I ... um ..."

"I see," Elisabeth nodded, remembering Mary's words about being newly betrothed.

Her cousin had a valid question. Why *had* Zacharias been struck deaf and dumb after his encounter with Gabriel, while Mary had remained untouched?

When the answer failed to come, Elisabeth shrugged. "I am afraid I do not know, Mary. Obviously the angel heard something different in your question than that of my husband. What that was, I cannot say. I suppose we shall have to ask Zacharias. In any case, as much as I would like to hear the end of your story, I feel it would be unfair to him." She rose from the chair.

Jacob also started to rise. "Would you like me to fetch—"

Shaking her head, Elisabeth stared at her cousins' dusty, sandaled feet, and gasped in horror. "Oh! A thousand apologies, Jacob. I do not know how I could have forgotten to offer water. Allow me to fetch a basin. I will be right back." Mortified that she had failed to wash their dust-covered feet, Elisabeth spun around, but Anna caught her arm.

"Don't be silly, Elisabeth. Of course we can't have you carrying around giant pots of water and bending over like that. Mary, you fetch the water while Jacob and I unload the cart. That should give Elisabeth enough time to explain our arrival to Zacharias."

Elisabeth smiled when the small family jumped to obey Anna's instructions. "Thank you, Anna. I greatly appreciate the help. If you will all excuse me for a moment, I will fetch Zacharias."

Elisabeth made her way into the small room Zacharias used as his study. Pausing in front of the doorway, she peeked in on her husband. He sat forward in his chair, his elbows resting on the desk and his cheeks in his hands. The scroll from which he read was held open by two large polished rocks weighing down the parchment. For a moment, she simply watched him.

The rich brown of his beard had long since turned from gray to white. The once smooth skin of his hands was now spotted and wrinkled with age. Notwithstanding the obvious advancement of years, shadows of the handsome young man he had once been still lingered on his kind, elderly face, and Elisabeth once again counted herself fortunate to have married such a wonderful man as this. His hair appeared as though he had been running his hands through it. She crossed to him, pushing her own fingers lightly through his thick, white mane.

She secretly delighted in the way his startled confusion shifted to joy when he turned to look up at her. Even now, despite being old and heavy with child, he could still gaze at her in a way that made her feel beautiful.

Reaching down for the ever-present parchment on the side of his desk, she dipped a pen in ink and scrawled *Jacob and his family are here. You should come out and greet them. Mary has some questions for you.*

Nodding, Zacharias took the pen from her. *Is this a coincidence or something more?*

He passed back the pen and, grinning, Elisabeth wrote, *Come out and see.*

With a smile and a shake of his head, he removed the polished rocks from the parchment and carefully rolled it up. Elisabeth gathered the ink, two pens, and several more sheets of parchment, knowing that they would likely need them all before the night was through. Zacharias motioned for her to lead the way. She stepped back out into the front room.

Mary knelt on the ground, washing her mother's feet as Jacob carried in the last of the food supplies, depositing them on the dining table.

Elisabeth stepped to the side in time for Zacharias to hurry past her to silently greet his kin. He gripped Jacob's arms in both of his, turning to hug Anna and then Mary. He reached down and gently tugged the cloth Mary was using out of her hand.

Elisabeth shrugged her shoulders when the young girl glanced up at her. "Go ahead and let him finish, child. Then we can catch up."

When Zacharias completed the cleansing ritual, he beamed at his guests. Wiping his still damp hands on his robes, he took the writing supplies from Elisabeth. Moving into the dining room, he beckoned for them all to follow. Elisabeth fell into line behind Mary and her parents. Together, they surrounded the small table.

Zacharias set down the pen and parchment before rearranging the items Jacob had deposited there only moments ago, until he had enough space to comfortably write.

Welcome to our home! I am so glad to see you all. Now, as you can plainly see, my methods of communication are severely limited. I am sure that

Elisabeth has already explained my current predicament and her own delicate condition, so I'll not waste your time or our parchment by covering the same ground. She has also told me that you come bearing news. I would love to hear about it.

When he finished, he lifted the second pen and handed it to Elisabeth. Though she felt a sudden urge to tell her husband about Mary's condition herself, Elisabeth instead passed the writing utensil off to Mary. When Mary hesitated, Elisabeth smiled her reassurance.

Nervously, the girl stepped forward and dipped the pen in the inkwell. She touched the tip to the parchment. With Elisabeth and her parents peering over her shoulder, she wrote in a neat flowing script. *Hello, cousin. I am sorry to hear of your ailments. I do hope you will recover quickly.*

Zacharias give a soundless chuckle as he pressed his pen to the paper in a much untidier scrawl than her own. *Don't you worry about that, child. I'll recover soon enough. This curse is of my own doing, but it is temporary, thank the Lord. I appreciate the niceties, but as you can see, on paper they leave a lot to be desired. Now, if you would please explain what tidings brought you and your parents to Hebron.*

One careful word at a time, Mary wrote of her miraculous visitation from the angel. Elisabeth read over Mary's shoulder and smiled when she read how the holy messenger comforted the girl by telling her that her cousin was also with child.

Elisabeth divided her attention between Mary's words and the growing excitement of her husband. Though she had already heard the story, it was somehow different as she read over Mary's shoulder, forcing her tired eyes to focus on the words. Her own excitement grew as she heard of the account a second time.

The joy lighting Zacharias' face as he stared at the parchment was infectious. Her heartbeat quickened. His head slowly inched toward it as though his proximity to the page could coax the words out of Mary's pen faster.

Elisabeth felt Zacharias briefly slip his arm around her waist as he read to the end of the account. They shared a happy smile before he gently took Mary's tiny, flawless hands in his own gnarled fists. Reverently, he kissed her palms, and Elisabeth could see the sheen of tears glistening in his eyes.

Letting go of the young girl, Zacharias picked up his pen. *Elisabeth mentioned something about a question. What is bothering you, child?*

Elisabeth told us you had been cursed for questioning the angel, Mary wrote. *I also questioned him, but he simply answered my questions.*

Zacharias grinned as he shook his head, showing that he understood. *Mary, our situations were completely different. Your question sprang from the innocence of youth. Gabriel saw it for what it was and answered in kind. The moment he answered, you reaffirmed your desire to follow the Lord in all things.*

I, on the other hand, am an old man. I have served in the temple for most of my life, and when Gabriel revealed that Elisabeth would conceive my first thought was to ask for a sign. An angel of God revealed a miracle to me, and I had the audacity to ask him for verification. I treated a holy messenger as if he were merely a man, and I was sharply reprimanded.

Believe it or not, I do not see my condition as unjust. My faith in the Lord has increased. I look forward to the day when my son will be born. When that day comes, I will regain my hearing and my speech. Until that time, I will serve my wife as well as I am able and dedicate my time to my God. I am not at all unpleased with my current circumstances.

As if inspiration lit Anna's mind, Mary's mother took the pen from her daughter. *Zacharias, would it help if Mary and I remained here until after the birth? We could be available to help in ways that you cannot.*

"I'm sorry, Jacob," Anna said as she faced her husband. "I've been thinking about this, ever since we walked in. I meant to approach you with it first, but ..."

Jacob shook his head in understanding. "There is no need, Anna. Had you not brought it up, I was prepared to. I only wish that I could stay and offer my services as well."

"Really, Mama?" Mary asked excitedly. "Do you mean it?"

"Only if they will have us. Elisabeth?" Anna turned to her. "I can only imagine how hard the last six months have been on you. If you consent, Mary and I will remain and help out as much as possible, and we would also be present to assist with the birth."

Elisabeth immediately felt her eyes burn. How could Anna have known that she had been praying for this? Though she never would have revealed it to her husband, she dreaded the final stages of the pregnancy. It had always been difficult for her to accept help from others, but the thought of having Mary and Anna here to help her through this difficult time was almost too good to be true.

"I don't ... quite know what to say," Elisabeth whispered, bringing a hand to her heart. "It would be a great comfort if the pair of you were to remain. Heaven knows that I am in need of the help, but I know your lives are in Nazareth. Three months is a long time to be away."

"Don't be silly, Elisabeth," Anna scolded gently. "We are family. Of course we will stay. This will also serve as a valuable teaching tool for Mary."

Feeling an enormous weight lift off of her shoulders, Elisabeth nodded. "In that case, your help and comfort would be most welcome and greatly appreciated."

CHAPTER 7

MARY

I s there anything else I can I get for you, Elisabeth?" Mary stepped next to the bedridden woman and handed her a cup of water. "Are you warm enough? Perhaps I could find you another—"

"No, child." Elisabeth's weary voice tugged at Mary's heartstrings. Mary guided her cousin's trembling hand to the cup and helped her bring the cool water to Elisabeth's chapped lips.

While the last three months had been difficult for Mary in many ways, it seemed paltry when compared to what her kinswoman had experienced. It was clear that Elisabeth's body had undoubtedly been strengthened by the Lord, but pregnancy was still taking its toll on the poor woman.

Not long after their arrival, Elisabeth began to experience heavy contractions and Anna, fearing an early delivery, had insisted her elderly cousin remain in bed as much as possible.

With Zacharias in his current state and her mother constantly tending to Elisabeth, most of the daily chores fell to Mary. In the beginning, it had not been too difficult. The elderly couple lived simply and did not expect much in the way of extravagances. Meals were modest, and because Zacharias spent his free time reading, messes were few and far between. During the early mornings, before the heat set in, Mary's mother would bring a chair out into the small garden of flowers Elisabeth cultivated in front of her house. Because Mary enjoyed the way Elisabeth's face would light up during her time amongst the blossoms, she took it upon herself to keep up the garden. It was an enjoyable pastime, and it gave her plenty of opportunities to converse with her cousin about their unborn children and what the future might be like once they arrived.

Most evenings she would sit with Zacharias in his study, and he would point out the prophecies that the prophets of old had written concerning the Savior. It felt so much different reading them now, knowing that the fruit of the prophecies was even now growing within her womb. The words of Isaiah especially called to her. Zacharias took great delight in pointing out the passages that spoke of a messenger who would precede the Son of God. She was astonished to discover that Isaiah had mentioned *her* specifically. He referred to her as 'the virgin' and the subtle reverence in the ancient prophet's writing humbled her.

During her second month in Hebron, Mary woke up feeling extremely ill. At first the sickness frightened her, but both Elisabeth and her mother quickly explained that the illness was common for many women in the early stages of pregnancy. It was simply her body's way of adjusting to all of the changes taking place in preparation for carrying a baby. Over the next few weeks, the nausea intensified. Mary resigned herself to carrying a bucket around wherever she went.

Once Elisabeth reached the point of immobility, Mary suggested to her mother that they place a few of the woman's flowers into various pots. Her idea was to rotate them in and out of the house so that Elisabeth might enjoy their beauty from the confines of her bed. After giving it a moment of thought, Anna acquiesced and Mary spent the afternoon in the garden carefully digging up a variety of bulbs and replanting them in the multiple clay pots that her cousin had scattered throughout the house. That evening, when they brought the flowers in, Elisabeth became ecstatic, overcome with joy and gratitude that she might still enjoy the comfort of her blossoms.

Zacharias, watching from the doorway, winked at Mary, flashing her a grateful smile.

As Elisabeth's time drew near, Mary made sure to observe closely. She knew that within a matter of months, the same changes would happen to her. She wanted to be as ready as possible for whatever she might experience. What she was not prepared for was the levels of pain her cousin endured. On more than one occasion, Elisabeth broke out in a cold sweat from the intensity of the contractions. Though the thought that she would one day soon suffer the same agonies scared her, Mary never wavered. She stuck by Elisabeth's side, determined to do all that was asked of her.

One morning as Mary sat in the front room, holding her bucket close and trying to avoid the smells of food coming from behind the house, her mother called out to her.

"Mary! Elisabeth's time has come. I need you, child!"

Extremely nauseous, Mary rose and stepped into the bedroom where her mother sat with a cloth draped over Elisabeth's sweaty brow. The elderly woman's hair was disheveled and slicked with sweat. Her face wore an expression of intense concentration. She sucked in short, clipped breaths, breathing out between pursed lips as she stared straight ahead.

Mary jumped when Elisabeth let out a wild shriek and squeezed her eyes shut, her hands grasping at her swollen belly.

"What can I do, Mama?" Mary asked, aching for her cousin.

"You must fetch the midwife," Anna answered. "You remember where she lives?"

Mary nodded, fighting the familiar urge to vomit.

"Will you be all right, Mary?" Anna questioned, a worried tone in her voice as she studied Mary's face. "You look pale."

"I'll be fine, Mama," Mary said as she turned to walk out of the room. "The sickness will pass. It always does. I will return soon with the midwife."

As she passed through the front room on the way to the door, Zacharias stopped her, pausing to peer into her face. Knowing she needed to hurry, Mary reached for the parchment he had tucked in one of the many pockets of his robes to write a quick explanatory note, but he waved her hands away. He signaled for her to sit down, but exasperated and queasy, Mary only shook her head. She tried pantomiming to him that Elisabeth was about to give birth, though the motions made her dizzy.

Zacharias nodded as though he understood, but he continued to point to the chair. Though a part of her wanted to rush past the old man, Mary knew full well how insistent he could be, so she took the seat. It was too difficult to fight both Zacharias and the growing nausea. The moment he left her alone, she could continue her errand.

Instead of leaving, Zacharias stepped behind her and placed his hands on her head. For a moment, Mary sat there, slightly bewildered. Then she closed her eyes and the nausea seemed to melt away. Her mind filled with clarity and purpose. She held very still as Zacharias finished the silent blessing. When he finished, she felt him remove his hands from her head. Standing, she turned to face him.

"Thank you," she whispered, slightly awed by his perceptivity.

For a moment she studied the righteous man, but a scream from the other room brought her back to her senses. *The midwife!*

"I have to go," she mouthed slowly, exaggerating the words and pointing to the street outside.

Zacharias nodded and sidestepped so she could access the front door. Not wasting any more time, and no longer burdened with morning sickness, Mary sprinted through the streets to the home of the midwife. Some of the villagers she had met during her three month visit waved and called out, but Mary was in too much of a hurry to answer. Hebron, nestled in the Judean mountains, was not a particularly flat town. Of course the midwife lived uphill from the home of Zacharias. It was not long before Mary's calves began to burn as she ran, but the knowledge that her cousin was in much more pain than she lent wings to her feet.

It took longer than she might have liked, but soon Mary found herself standing at the entryway of the midwife, huffing and puffing as she tried to regain her breath. Lifting an arm, she knocked on the heavy, wooden door. A quick glance at the position of the sun told Mary that it was still early, and she hoped the woman had not already been called away. Fortunately, she heard a shuffling from inside and the door swung open to reveal the stout, middle-aged frame of the midwife.

"Ah! Good morning, child. How are you this fine day?"

"I … am … doing well, thank you," Mary panted.

"That is wonderful to hear," the midwife said with a smile. "What brings you up here, young Mary, and in such an exhausted state?" She looked her up and down with a shrewd and knowing expression. "You should really exercise more caution, my dear. You must think of the child."

Mary stared up in horror. She hadn't told anybody about her pregnancy. How could this woman possibly know?

"I am a midwife, girl!" the woman reminded her. "Did you not think I would recognize a woman with child when she stands at my own threshold? I assumed that you did not wish to discuss it, and the circumstances are none of my business. When the time comes, should you choose to bear the baby here in Hebron, I will be here. You just send for old Miriam and I'll come running." Mary nodded in appreciation grateful for the woman's kind words.

"I assume since you are here," she continued, stepping back into the confines of her house, "Elisabeth is ready to deliver." Again she clucked her tongue. "Imagine, a woman at her age giving birth. God works in mysterious ways, indeed."

Re-emerging, she had one arm wrapped around a large wicker basket filled to the brim with clay bottles, bandages, sponges, woolen wraps, and other assorted items. In the other hand, she held a U-shaped stool.

"Well," she said, handing the stool to Mary and reaching behind to shut her door. "Let us be on our way. We have a busy day ahead of us."

Though Mary still felt the sense of urgency, Miriam would not be rushed. "Do not worry, child. The birthing process takes many hours," she chuckled when Mary tried to pick up their pace. You will not miss it. I have no desire to take a headfirst tumble down this mountainside."

After what seemed like ages to Mary, they arrived at the home of Elisabeth. Finding the door closed, Mary knocked hard, shifting the heavy stool in her grip so she would not drop it. To her surprise, Aaron, the handsome young friend of Zacharias, answered the door. Blushing slightly at the sight of Mary, he held it open for the two women.

"Ah, yes," he said, stepping aside so they could move past him and into the house. "Welcome, Miriam. Anna and Elisabeth will be most pleased to see you."

Miriam gave a curt nod of greeting before bustling into the house, making a beeline for Elisabeth's bedroom.

"Hi, Aaron," Mary said, following after the determined midwife. "I am sure Zacharias will be glad of your company today."

"Yes, of course," he mumbled, the blush deepening as his glance flickered from her to the floor and back again. "Give my best to Elisabeth."

"I will. Thank you."

Mary followed Miriam and, after shutting the door behind her, she set the stool on the ground with a sigh of relief. Reaching up, she massaged her upper arms. *Just looking at it, you wouldn't think it was that heavy,* she thought, turning her attention to Elisabeth.

Her mother gripped one of the elderly woman's legs and massaged slowly as the midwife stepped forward to begin her examination.

"Mary, take the other leg," Anna said with authority. "Start with the foot and work your way up. Let's try to keep her as relaxed as possible."

"Yes, Mama. I understand."

For the next several hours, Mary alternated between massaging, continually refilling pitchers of water, wiping Elisabeth down with damp towels to remove the sweat, and anything else that her mother or the midwife demanded. Occasionally, Miriam demanded that Elisabeth stand up and walk around the room. Mary and her mother would each take a side and support her as she hobbled in small circles around the bed until the midwife instructed her to return.

As the day wore on, Mary became increasingly grateful for the blessing Zacharias had given her earlier. She could not imagine trying to do this while nauseous. Even as she worked, Mary prayed for her cousin, asking that God might have mercy on her and help her to deliver a healthy baby. She cringed a little more each time a contraction hit. *I don't know how she bears it,* Mary thought, rubbing the woman's belly, which became as hard as a rock with each contraction. *I don't know how I am going to bear it.*

Finally, the midwife announced that the time had come. The baby was ready to be delivered. Between contractions, Mary and Anna helped Elisabeth stagger over to the U-shaped stool. Each of them took a side to help her keep her balance.

"Hold a knee, ladies," Miriam ordered, taking her position at the rear of the stool, near the U. She reached into the basket and pulled out a large pillow which she set to the side of the chair. "She will need to use you for leverage as she pushes. Elisabeth, I want you to pay close attention to your body. Though you are in remarkably good health for your age, there are still risks here. Your body is ready to deliver this baby, but you need to stay in tune with it. If done right, your own body will tell you when to push. Bear down for as long and as hard as feels natural and stop when you need to breathe. Use your contractions as a guide."

The midwife continued to murmur gentle instructions as Elisabeth nodded anxiously. Mary reached up and gently massaged her cousin's shoulder as she tried desperately to commit everything to memory. Taking a deep breath, Elisabeth sat forward in the stool, resting her elbows on both Mary's and Anna's shoulders. Mary winced when she pushed down but held her ground, wanting to give Elisabeth all of the support she needed.

The midwife was indeed skilled in her craft, and it did not take long before a screaming baby lay on the pillow, his hands and feet flailing about feebly as he cried. Anna bundled him up as the midwife helped Elisabeth through the final stages of the birth. Mary assisted her mother in cleaning the baby.

"You can help Elisabeth now." The midwife stood up from her crouched position and nodded to Mary and her mother. "She is exhausted and needs to rest. I'll tend to the babe." Miriam held out her hands over a large basin. Understanding what she wanted, Mary picked up a pitcher of water pouring it over the midwife's hands and arms. Picking up a fresh towel, Miriam patted herself dry before holding her arms out expectantly.

Anna deposited the wriggling baby into them and motioned for Mary to grip Elisabeth's opposite side. Together, they half-carried the trembling Elisabeth to her bed. When she could sit, Anna helped Elisabeth slide into position and Mary lifted her cousin's legs and swung them onto the bed. For a moment, the cries of the baby sounded strangely garbled. Mary looked up in time to see the midwife run a gentle finger into his mouth to clear out the fluids. When Miriam finished, she softly sponged him off with warm water. Mary, studying the tiny purple body, was surprised to see how elongated the head was.

"It is only temporary," Miriam said when she saw Mary staring. "His head will take on a normal shape within a matter of days."

"He … has so much hair." Mary said with a smile.

"Yes, he is just like his father, although there is a chance that most of the hair will fall out and he will regrow it. Now, would you like to help me clean him up?"

Mutely, Mary nodded, watching as the baby's skin continued to transition from purple to pink.

"Come over here. Reach into the basket for a second sponge and dip it into the water. You can start with his feet and work your way up while I work from the head down."

When they finished, Miriam showed Mary how to take the long strips of swaddling cloth and wrap the baby snugly in them so that he would feel safe and secure.

With a contented smile, the midwife deposited the baby into Mary's arms. "You've done well, child. Now, why don't you hand him to Elisabeth? I am sure she would like to hold her son."

It took Elisabeth a few days to recover. During that time, Mary spent many hours caring for her tiny cousin. At first, the baby was fairly tranquil, wanting nothing more than to sleep and eat. By the end of the first week, however, she was amazed with how alert and active he had become. He constantly kicked against the swaddling clothes, and somehow he always managed to pull his arms free. It did not take Mary long to become fully proficient in the art of wrapping.

Though the baby was a wonder, what was truly miraculous was Elisabeth's recovery. On the sixth morning, the elderly woman surprised Mary and her mother by shoving back the covers and announcing that she was going outside and breathe in the morning air and greet her flower garden.

Mary caught Zacharias' eye. They both grinned as Elisabeth ignored Anna's sputtering protests, marching out of the room and through the front door.

In that moment, Mary knew that her visit to Hebron was rapidly drawing to a close. The idea of returning to Nazareth both thrilled and terrified her. She desperately longed to see her father again. She wanted to feel the familiar comfort of her own bed and the solitude of her own room. Most of all, she ached to see Joseph and feel his arms around her. She was sure that her father had explained her long absence to him, but would he forgive her for leaving so abruptly? And there was the matter of her secret … the secret that only her parents, Zacharias, and Elisabeth knew, the secret that would not remain so for much longer. *How am I going to tell him?* Even as she asked herself the question, she knew the answer.

She would tell him the truth, nothing more and nothing less. Joseph would either accept it … or he would not.

On the morning of the eighth day after the birth of her cousin's baby, Mary stood near her mother as Elisabeth and Zacharias welcomed the mohel into their home. The front room was crowded with family, friends, and neighbors there to witness the circumcision and naming of the baby. It was a fortunate coincidence for the family that the mohel, the man trained to perform the circumcision, just happened to be Daniel, a nephew of Zacharias. Knowing how special this ceremony was for their cousins, Mary and Anna chose to stay out of the way as the rite was performed. Mary felt a pang of sadness when the baby screamed out in obvious pain, but her mother rested a comforting hand on her shoulder.

"This is a commandment of the Lord, Mary." Anna whispered in her ear. "It is right that his forerunner should be subject to it. Steel yourself now, for it will be more difficult when your own child lies in the hands of the mohel. Remember the blessings that come through righteous obedience to the Lord's council."

"I understand, Mama," Mary said quietly. "I would have it no other way."

When the ritual was complete and the baby rested in the arms of Zacharias, questions began to circulate about the child's name.

Daniel raised his arms and the murmuring ceased. He held out an inviting hand to Aaron, the priest officiating over the ceremony.

Stepping forward reverently, Aaron carefully took the baby from Zacharias. "The time has come to name the child. I propose that from this day forward, he be called Zacharias, in honor of the father. Zacharias has always been a humble and honest man. A man dedicated to God, and it is only right that the child should carry—"

To the amazement of all, Elisabeth stepped forward. "No. I am sorry, Aaron, but the child's name is John."

Aaron's mouth opened in surprise as murmuring filled the room. "But, Elisabeth. Neither you nor your husband has any kindred that are called by this name. Surely, you—"

When Elisabeth gave a stubborn shake of her head, Aaron turned to Zacharias. The old man frowned slightly, as though he were trying to follow the conversation. Mary watched the young priest shift the baby so that he could cradle him in one arm before making a series of gestures to the old man.

Zacharias pulled a slip of parchment out of his robe, and dipped a quill in a nearby pot of ink, he quickly scrawled something on the thin material and handed it to Aaron.

The young man studied the writing carefully before turning to the rest of the congregation.

He glanced down at the scrap one more time before clearing his throat. "His name is John."

Just after Aaron read the name, Zacharias stepped forward boldly and took the baby from the officiating priest. Surprised at first, Aaron quickly stepped back to give Zacharias the floor. For a moment, the old man gazed down into the child's eyes with loving adoration. Then he looked up, his eyes bright and clear, and opened his mouth.

Mary's eyebrows furrowed in confusion, not at all sure what her cousin was doing. He could not talk. So why was he acting as though he were going to address the people?

And then she understood.

Words poured from Zacharias' mouth. The phrases were rich and full, not at all raspy or hoarse. This was not the voice of a man who had been silent for nine months. The elderly priest sounded as though he had been conversing only moments before.

Loud and clear Zacharias announced, "Blessed be the Lord God of Israel; for he hath visited and redeemed his people, and hath raised up a horn of salvation for us in the house of his servant David; as he spake by the mouth of his holy prophets, which have been since the world began: that we should be saved from our enemies, and from the hand of all that hate us; to perform the mercy promised to our fathers, and to remember his holy covenant; the oath which he sware to our father Abraham, that he would grant unto us, that we being delivered out of the hands of our enemies might serve him without fear, in holiness and righteousness before him, all the days of our life."

Mary put her hands to her breast as she listened to the words of the kindly old man. He spoke pure prophecy—the same nature of prophecy that she had read with him night after night. These were the words of the Holy Ghost.

All around her the people stood silent, hanging on each word Zacharias pronounced.

"And thou, child," he said, staring down at his tiny son, still held in the crook of his arm, "shalt be called the prophet of the Highest: for thou shalt go before the face of the Lord to prepare his ways; to give knowledge of salvation unto his people by the remission of their sins, through the tender mercy of our God; whereby the dayspring from on high hath visited us, to give light to them that sit in darkness and in the shadow of death, to guide our feet into the ways of peace!"

CHAPTER 8

JOSEPH

Joseph stared angrily at the faulty boards stacked in a haphazard fashion near the door to his shop. With a growl of frustration, he dropped the long, slender piece of lumber he carried. It clattered to the wooden floor, shattering on impact. The entire batch was rotten to the point of being unusable. He needed this load to finish the benches that would match the table currently occupying the display platform near the window.

Kicking his way through the broken wood, Joseph ran a hand along one of the legs of the table.

"This piece turned out well enough," he muttered critically. "Not that it matters without the benches." Now, he would have to notify his customers that he would require additional time.

He hated coming in late on projects. Even in Nazareth, there was too much competition in the field of carpentry to risk upsetting loyal buyers by failing to deliver when promised. He would most likely be forced to return a percentage of the down payment he had received, and he was barely making a profit on the set as it was. Joseph bit down on his lip to keep the angry words on the tip of his tongue from escaping. The trip to his supplier would take the better part of the day, and after that, he would need to explain to the blacksmith and his family why their new dining set would be delayed.

With a sigh, he moved to the small desk near the back of the shop where he conducted his business negotiations. He opened one of the drawers, pulled out a small sealed box, and set it on the desk in front of him. Withdrawing a slim, silver key from his robes, he slid it into the lock on the cashbox and turned it. With a faint click, the lock disengaged and Joseph lifted the lid. Glancing at the stacks of small coins and promissory notes, Joseph pulled out a tiny coin pouch. After a moment's hesitation, he pulled out a handful of other coins as well, dropping them into the purse before cinching it shut. Hefting it in his hand a couple of times, he sighed and slipped it into a pocket sewn into his girdle. He closed the box and locked it tight, testing the lid to make certain it was secure.

Carefully, he reset the lock on the cashbox and tucked it back into his desk. When he was sure that all was secure, Joseph walked to his shop's entrance and pushed open the door. Glaring at the rotten wood once more, he picked up one piece he could use as proof and pulled a key from his pocket to lock the door. Just as the lock clicked, the carpenter heard the one sound that had the power to turn his entire day around.

"Joseph!"

Through the haze of temper, Joseph felt his lips curve upward. Spinning around, he turned to face the woman to whom he had given his heart. He dropped the rotten piece of wood and opened his arms so Mary could fling herself into them.

"Mary!" he said, pushing his own troubles to the back of his mind as he twirled her. "You're back!"

Then, noticing the disapproving glances from the passersby, he quickly put her down and took a step back.

"I am *so* sorry," she whispered, reaching a hand up to clutch at her shawl. "I only meant to be gone for a couple of days. It was only supposed to be a small—"

"Beloved," he said gently. "Your father explained it all to me. I understand. I would not have had it any other way. I missed you every day, but I know what it means to help a family member in need."

"Oh, Joseph! I missed you, too! The whole time! It made my heart ache to be separated from you for so long."

Joseph placed a calloused hand on her cheek. "Well, you are back now. And in only a few more short months, we will be married."

He felt her tremble slightly even as she reached up and tentatively cupped his hand with her own. When she nodded, it made his heart pound a little faster.

"I have so many things I need to tell you. There is so much you should know. Can we go into your shop?"

Joseph flicked his eyes to the door he had just locked. "That might not be the best idea," he said, considering the mess of rotten wood scattered all over the floor. "I'll tell you what. I was about to run some errands. Due to the nature of them, I would be most appreciative of good company. Perhaps you could tell me about your time in Hebron as we walk?"

He paused and studied at her seriously for a moment before giving an extravagant bow. "That is, if you would be so good as to grant me the honor of your companionship."

With a giggle, Mary dropped an answering curtsy. "The pleasure would be mine, master carpenter."

Chuckling, Joseph reached down to pick up the discarded board before starting down the street. Though he was still prepared to have words with the supplier, perhaps, with Mary present, things would not grow quite so heated.

"Where are we going?" Mary asked, stepping up beside him.

"My wood supplier is located south of the city, about an hour's walk from here. My latest shipment was delivered this morning and it is … well, let's just say it is unusable. In any case, I needed that wood to finish a project. Due to the quality of the boards, I must also notify my customer that their dining set will be delayed."

"Ooh," Mary said, her lower lip between her teeth. "That can't be good."

"No, it's not," Joseph agreed. "I can only hope that the smith is having a good day. However, I did not invite you along so that you could listen to my business problems. Tell me all about what has happened since your departure. I trust you found your cousin well?"

As though a dam had burst, words poured from the young girl in an excited flood.

Joseph listened in fascination to Mary's account of what happened in the mountains of Hebron. He was not sure he believed everything she told him about this strange priestly cousin being struck deaf and dumb one minute and miraculously recovering the next, but she was so caught up in the story that he decided not to interrupt. As she spoke, he noticed that she absently toyed with a lock of her long hair, repeatedly lifting it toward her mouth before dropping it. Could it be that she was nervous to see him? But that was nonsense! They were betrothed. Trying to dismiss the thoughts, Joseph focused on what she was saying.

Just outside of the edge of town, Joseph saw a group of people slowly shuffling on the road toward them. At first he thought nothing of it, but then he caught the tinkling sound of bells. Quickly, he pulled Mary off to the side of the road.

"Lepers," he warned, walking with her into the brush.

Her eyes sad, Mary nodded and allowed him to lead her away from the main road. Though the sight of lepers was not uncommon, Joseph was touched with his young bride-to-be's compassion for the poor souls. Knowing that he could ill-afford the charity, Joseph nonetheless hurried back to the road and opened his purse. He pulled out the extra coins he had belatedly added earlier and stacked them in a neat stack on the side of the road before hurrying back to where Mary waited.

"That was very thoughtful," Mary said taking his arm and gazing directly into his eyes. "Thank you, Joseph."

A little embarrassed by her praise, Joseph nodded. The disease-stricken individuals approached. As they neared, Joseph saw six small children in the midst of the group, and his heart ached for them. Most of the lepers stumbled by without meeting their eyes or glancing in their direction. When one of the young children grew even with the coins, she looked over at them with large, somber eyes that had seen and experienced more than any child should have to bear. Blood-stained wrappings covered her head and face, but they drooped in places and Joseph could see the open sores and lumps that accompanied the disease.

Fighting back the gut-wrenching pity, Joseph gave her a tiny smile and made a slight gesture to the ground where he had set the coins. Obviously startled by the fact that he was looking right at her, the girl gawked at him. Again, Joseph motioned to the money, and slowly, her eyes followed his pointing finger to the ground.

Joseph could not help but squeeze Mary's hand when the child discovered the coins. With a squeal of delight, she carefully reached down with one bandaged hand and picked up the money.

He watched as the girl hurried to one of the women in the group and showed her the coins. The woman's eyes grew big as she caught the glint of metal and she asked the girl a question that Joseph could not hear. The child answered and pointed to where Joseph and Mary stood waiting.

When the woman's haunted eyes fixed on them, Joseph saw streaks in the dust that covered her face. She lifted a hand in gratitude and Joseph answered by lifting his own in silent farewell.

Together he and Mary waited for the group of lepers to pass before making their way back to the road. For a time, neither of them spoke. Joseph's thoughts turned back to the things that Mary had been telling him before.

Peering at the countryside, he pondered her story. The story of this aging priest sounded ludicrous. Sure, the ancient prophets wrote of miracles and angelic visitations, but that was so long ago. He always considered himself a spiritual man, but even to his open mind, Mary's account seemed farfetched. Casting a sidelong glance at his soon-to-be bride, Joseph was suddenly struck with the realization of how young she really was. Though he was well aware of her intelligence, she was still a girl, only beginning to make the transition into womanhood. Like most Hebrew women her age, she held her elders in high regard and her mind was still impressionable. Silently, he could not help wondering if she had simply gotten carried away in the romanticism of her cousin's story.

"So, this priest claims to have been struck completely deaf and dumb," Joseph asked doubtfully, "and he was healed the moment his child was named?"

The sudden break in the silence seemed to surprise Mary. When Joseph saw the flicker of hurt in her eyes before she cast them toward the dirt, he wished he could take back his words.

"You … don't believe me?" she questioned in a small voice.

"Mary, it isn't really that I …" Joseph protested, but then fell silent. The truth was that he was not sure that he *did* believe her story. The thought of an angel coming to tell a man that his wife was going to have a baby was the stuff of stories. It just did not happen anymore.

For a long moment, Joseph stood studying the lovely face of the young girl he would one day marry. He wanted to say something, comforting but he had no idea what. Before he could think of something, Mary raised her head, and met his gaze. Joseph was surprised by the fierce intensity and absolute conviction in those beautiful eyes. Her stare challenged him. Joseph wanted to look away, but he found himself trapped, helpless to avert his eyes.

"Joseph," she said, not breaking eye contact, "I am with child."

Joseph's jaw dropped as he gaped at the woman that would have been his wife. As his heart stopped in his chest, he hoped he had heard her wrong. *How could she be with child? We are betrothed. We are set to be married!*

"B-but—" Joseph sputtered.

Mary stood straighter, her countenance stronger somehow. Her words clear and direct.

"The night after our betrothal, I was preparing myself for bed when I saw a brilliant, white light in the middle of my room. In the midst of that light, I heard a voice call me by my name. An angel appeared to me, Joseph. He told me that I was to be the mother of the Son of God."

Standing in the street, Joseph listened with growing skepticism. "But we aren't married yet …" Joseph argued, hoping that this might be some kind of horrible joke.

"My child is the *Son of God*, Joseph." Mary's quiet words, pierced his ears and heart at the same time.

Joseph broke eye contact and glared at the ground. His brain tried to process her words and a logical explanation worked its way to the surface. *You've been gone for three months in the hill country of Hebron. Of course the young men there would have been fascinated with your beauty. Mary, I thought you were stronger than that.*

Sick in his heart at the idea of Mary's betrayal, Joseph shifted his eyes back to her perfect face. He could see the shimmer of tears under her long dark lashes, and even through his own heartache, he wanted to reach out and brush them away before they could spill down her cheeks.

Why would you try to hide behind a ridiculous story? Can you not see how impossible it sounds? Was this the cause for the long delay in Hebron? Why couldn't you have simply told me the truth?

Then, for the first time, Joseph thought about the consequence of Mary's infidelity.

It was within his rights as her future husband to put her to death for this betrayal. If he so chose, he could have her stoned. Was she making up this crazy story in an effort to save her own life? He hoped that she knew him better than that.

While the idea that she had been unfaithful to him hurt Joseph deeply, he did not want to see her punished. As his hopes and dreams for a quiet future with the young girl shattered, he found himself reluctant to cause her any more pain than absolutely necessary.

"Please, Joseph," she pleaded brokenheartedly. "Please believe me."

Joseph shook his head, corralling his rising anger. "I'm sorry, Mary, but I can't."

Firming his resolve, he met her eyes once more. Though the expression of anguish on her face pierced straight into his heart, he gritted his teeth.

"I would never hurt you, Mary. Even now, knowing you have done this to me, I would never want to see you in pain."

"Joseph, you—"

Not sure how much longer he could hold onto his resolve, Joseph held a hand up to silence her. "I need time to think. I will come to your house soon, and we will discuss the betrothal annulment. Though I cannot stop the gossip from spreading as your time approaches, I will not fan the flames by publicly condemning you. Now go. Notify Jacob that he may expect me on the day following the Sabbath. Prepare yourself and your family for what is to come as best as you are able. I have business that I must attend to."

For what he expected to be the last time, Joseph looked into her now tear-ravaged face. Even in her grief, she was heartbreakingly beautiful. He tried to picture her the day he first met her outside the cobbler shop, but Joseph knew that this broken image of his first love would forever haunt him when he thought of what could have been. For a tragic moment they both stood immovable, their eyes locked in silent anguish.

Then Mary turned and fled back down the road the way they had come.

With a heavy heart, Joseph glowered at the long piece of wood gripped in his hand. His fingers tightened over the board, and for a moment he held the wild desire to smash it to the hardened dirt below. Instead, he took a deep breath … and then a second.

He still had work to do. He wanted nothing more than to return to his shop and lose himself in his craft, but Joseph placed one careful foot in front of the other and continued down the road to the lumberyard.

Tired and depressed, Joseph trudged back toward his shop on heavy feet. The day had gone from bad to worse after Mary left him standing alone on the country road. Instead of his usual tactful and calm demeanor, he allowed his temper to get the best of him during his discussion with his wood supplier. Joseph still could not believe how close he came to completely severing negotiations with the man before regaining control of himself. He always lived by the rule that business should not mix with personal problems, but today he had not been able to help himself.

In the end, the supplier reluctantly agreed to replace the rotten shipment. Due to an increase in orders and the approaching Sabbath, however, the replacement wood could not be delivered until the beginning of next week. Far from satisfied, Joseph agreed with the terms. After his original outburst, the wood supplier had been in no mood to do Joseph any favors. Although furious with the whole situation, Joseph could not honestly say that he blamed the man.

Upon returning to town, Joseph paid a visit to the smithy. It was the only highlight in an otherwise dismal afternoon. The smith, hammer and tongs in hand, had been understandably frustrated with the situation, but he understood Joseph's predicament and refused to take back the advance money. Just as Joseph prepared to leave, the blacksmith's wife and three-year-old daughter stopped by the shop, and the young girl presented Joseph with a wild rose she had picked on the way.

Standing still as a wooden post, Joseph studied the red petals attached to the long green stem. The vibrant array of colors appealed to him. As he looked at the natural perfection of the flower, Joseph thought of Mary. All through the afternoon, he wrestled with the hurt and anger of her betrayal, but he still could not get her words out of his head. *The baby is the Son of God, Joseph. The ... Son ... of ... GOD.*

When he reached his shop, Joseph placed a hand on the door. He knew he needed to go in. Other projects needed his attention, and there was still the matter of the rotten wood. He needed to dispose of it and sweep the floor. As he considered all the work waiting for him inside, Joseph also realized he was done for the day. There was nothing in his shop that could not wait until after the Sabbath.

At this moment, all he wanted was to be back in the comfort and solitude of his own house. The last thing he needed was to be approached by another customer.

Dropping his hand, Joseph turned away from the shop. Nazareth was not a large town, but many people were out and about trying to finish all of their errands prior to sundown and the beginning of the Sabbath Day. Having no desire to converse with anyone, Joseph kept his eyes down as he threaded his way through the streets in the direction of his home.

He knew his mother and father should be apprised of his decision to annul the engagement with Mary, but her words kept reverberating in his head. All the way home, the young girl's story replayed itself in his mind over and over followed by a single question. *What if she were telling the truth?* No, he would wait until the next day to talk with his parents.

All he wanted for now was to be alone at home.

Perhaps if I could simply fall into bed, I will awaken in the morning and find that the whole day has been nothing more than a bad dream.

"Joseph."

Hearing his name, Joseph's eyes popped open. He was immediately assaulted by an intensely bright light. Squinting, he lifted a hand to his brow and tried to determine who spoke to him. The light emanated from somewhere over the center of his bed. Confused and disoriented, Joseph squinted into the white glare.

"Joseph, thou son of David," a gentle male voice said, soothingly. "Fear not to take unto thee Mary thy wife: for that which is conceived in her is of the Holy Ghost."

Even as he stared incredulously into the brightness, Mary's words filled his mind. Is this what she had seen? Was this the angel who spoke to her? Joseph opened his mouth to speak, but before he could, the voice continued.

"And she shall bring forth a son, and thou shalt call his name JESUS: for he shall save his people from their sins. Now all this was done that it might be fulfilled which was spoken of the Lord by the prophet, saying, behold, a virgin shall be with child, and bring forth a son, and they shall call his name Emmanuel."

Joseph sat up in bed, rubbing his eyes. *Was it a dream?* he asked himself, searching the semidarkness for the bright light he saw only moments before.

"Hello," he called out tentatively. "Is anyone there?"

He was not sure if he were disappointed or relieved when he received no answer. One thing was certain— whether the vision was a dream or real, Joseph believed what the angel told him. With a great sigh of relief, Joseph felt his troubled heart grow lighter.

Mary had not betrayed him after all!

As incredulous as it all sounded, she was truly carrying the Son of God in her womb.

Lamplight still flickered, casting a soft glow over his room. His gaze settled on the rose, now lying on his dresser. Though his mind reeled from the implications of what he had heard, Joseph reached for one of the blocks of wood on the nightstand beside his bed and the sharp whittling knife next to it.

For the rest of the night, Joseph worked feverishly on the carving. Not caring about the wood shavings that filled his bed, he whittled away at the block until the image he saw in his mind began to take shape in the soft wood. As he carved, prayers of thanksgiving filled his heart. His beloved had remained true to him.

His faith restored, Joseph made plans for the future. Naturally, they would push the wedding up, although it must now be a private affair. Perhaps if they were discreet enough, the people of Nazareth might just believe he had gone up to Hebron and married her there. That rumor might keep the gossipmongers from whispering about Mary behind her back. Of course, he would have to tell his parents, but it might not be a bad thing to allow the Nazarenes to think that this child was his for now. He knew that it would be up to Mary to decide how much to reveal and to whom. He owed her that and so much more.

As the sun lit the morning sky, Joseph made a decision. He finished applying the last coat of polish to his carving.

Inspecting his creation one last time, Joseph tucked it in a clean polishing cloth and shoved back the covers. More than anything, he wanted to talk to Mary. He had to apologize for doubting her. He needed to make plans with Jacob and his father. So much needed to be done, and he could almost feel the time dribbling through his fingers.

Knowing it was the Sabbath, Joseph skimmed his fingers past his standard working robes and settled on the dark formal attire he reserved for holy day worship. Still deep in thought, he dressed quickly and prepared himself a simple bowl of fruit. He thought about what Mary had told him, and the angel's confirmation. Joseph was ashamed that his pride had allowed him to dismiss Mary's words so easily. He had been so convinced of her infidelity that he had not even attempted to discover the truth of her words.

How will she receive me?

For a time, Joseph continued to chastise himself, but the idea that the literal Son of God grew under his beloved's heart and would soon walk the Earth overwhelmed his thoughts. While he was passingly familiar with prophecies from his time spent in the synagogue, he now wished he had personal access to the sacred writings. He found himself thirsty for more knowledge about the birth of this Messiah. He wanted to study the words of Isaiah, Micah, and Jeremiah.

The vision he experienced the night before gave a sense of urgency to the prophet's words that had always eluded him before.

Unable to stand it any longer, Joseph pushed back his chair. Picking up the cloth containing the carving, he inspected it once more before tucking it into a pocket of his robes. Not wanting to waste more time, he exited the house and locked the front door. It wasn't until he reached the street that he hesitated. A sudden bout of nerves at the idea of facing Mary had him gazing longingly in the direction of the synagogue.

He nearly took the coward's way out, but knowing it would only make things more difficult if he waited, Joseph instead made for the home of Jacob. Along the way, he feverishly thought about how he might mend the damage that his mistrust created. He rejected idea after idea until he realized in panic that he was standing at the door to Mary's home. *What can I possibly tell her?* he asked himself hopelessly. Without any idea of what he was going to say, Joseph took a deep breath and rapped sharply on the wooden planks.

When Jacob answered, Joseph swallowed hard.

"Good Sabbath, Joseph," he said softly. "Mary told us to expect you tomorrow."

"Um … good Sabbath, sir," Joseph floundered. "I … ah … wonder if I might have a word with Mary."

Jacob leaned against the doorframe but did not break eye contact with him. "What is it that you want, Joseph? Mary is in a lot of pain right now, and I'd rather spare her from more. It would be better if you and my cousin simply came back tomorrow. We can take care of this unpleasantness once and for all at that time. I see no need to bring Mary any more anguish than is absolutely necessary."

Jacob straightened and started to close the door.

Joseph threw caution to the wind. "Cousin, please! I know I hurt Mary, but I have come to make things right. I beg you, just give me a chance to talk to her. If, once I am finished, she still wants me to leave, I will."

For a long moment, Jacob held the door still, as though weighing Joseph's words against his need to protect his daughter.

Joseph reached a nervous hand into the pocket of his robes and ran his fingers over the carving.

"Joseph." Jacob grunted a reluctant sigh. "You have no idea how much you have hurt my child. She could not sleep last night and neither I nor my wife have been able to stop her tears. I am sure you can understand my hesitancy in this."

"Jacob, I—"

"However," Mary's father said holding up a hand, "I am fully aware of the law. I know what is in your power to do to my daughter and my family. I know of many men that would have indulged in their anger and bitterness. Because, even in your anger you chose to show mercy to my little girl, I will allow this." He stepped back from the open door.

Feeling extremely ashamed, Joseph muttered a quiet "Thank you" and shuffled his feet.

"Wait here. I will see if Mary wishes to speak with you." Jacob pushed the front door open. "I cannot promise more than that."

"Thank you, Jacob," Joseph answered. "I ask nothing more."

With a nod, Jacob disappeared into his home.

Joseph reached into his pocket and gripped the soft cloth covering the carving. *Please, Mary,* he thought fiercely as a piece of the wood bit into his hand through the soft material. *Please come.*

For a long moment, Joseph stood there, pleading silently that Mary might appear. Finally, hanging his head in resignation, he released the carving and turned away, not at all sure what he would do next.

"Joseph?" a soft, melodious voice asked.

Joseph spun around. Mary stood before him, angelic and vulnerable. Her face was pale and her eyes were red and bloodshot, but he could not remember the last time he had seen something quite so lovely.

"Mary!" he breathed, unable to contain the relief that slid through him as he spoke her name. "I didn't think you were going to come out."

Mary stood as still as any of the countless chairs he had carved. The level of discomfort rose, causing Joseph to cough and clear his throat.

"Mary," he said finally, "I am not sure where to start. I don't know how to begin telling you how sorry I am."

Mary sucked in a breath, but before she could speak, Joseph hurried on.

"I found something in myself yesterday that I am not proud of. In my anger and frustration, I allowed fear and jealousy to get the better of me. Instead of opening my mind to the possibilities of the miracle you shared with me, I rejected your words and assumed the worst. I betrayed your trust and in so doing, I discovered a weakness in my own faith."

He looked directly into her tear-filled gaze, his own eyes wet and imploring. "I sincerely apologize for hurting you, Mary. I was impulsive and rash, and I have come to beg your forgiveness. If you will still take me as your husband, I will work every day to be worthy of the honor and privilege."

"Why, Joseph?" Mary swiped at her cheeks with the back of her hand. "Why this change of heart? What made you change your mind?"

"I am not quite sure how to explain it. I went to bed last night full of doubt and sadness, but I was awoken by a voice. When I opened my eyes, a light floated directly over my bed. Within that light stood a man. He radiated glory and power such as I have never known, and he told me that I should not be afraid to take you as my wife. He—" Joseph's voice broke. He wiped away his own tears. "He said that the child within you was conceived of the Holy Ghost," he whispered. "He said that this child should be named Jesus and that he would one day save the world from their sins."

"Oh, Joseph!" Mary rushed forward to wrap her arms around him. "I'm so glad you believe me. I prayed for this every night while I was with Elisabeth!"

"I'm just sorry that it took an angel to convince me of the truth of your words, my beloved," he answered, gently cupping her cheeks in his calloused hands. "I will not doubt you again."

"So what do we do now?" his beautiful bride-to-be asked.

"I think we should marry as quickly as possible," Joseph answered. "The ceremony should be done in secret. We could let it be whispered that I visited you in Hebron and we were married there. If we are discreet, people will assume the baby is mine for now, and it would avoid a lot of unpleasant gossip. What do you think?"

"I think that sounds absolutely wonderful!"

Joseph sighed in relief to hear the giddy excitement back in her voice.

"Come on," she said, grabbing his hand and pulling him toward the house. "Let's go and tell my father!"

"Mary, wait," he answered, stopping her. "Before we go in, there is one more thing."

Reaching into his pocket, he pulled out the cloth containing the carving. Delicately, he folded back a corner of the cloth and presented her with the wooden rose he had painstakingly created.

"Joseph! It's beautiful!"

"I couldn't go back to sleep after the visitation," he said quietly. "Yesterday I was given a rose by the blacksmith's daughter. Every time I saw it, I could only think of you." He stroked the oil-rubbed petals fondly. "You are my rose, Mary. I wanted to give you something to show you how much you mean to me."

Mary gifted him with the small, intimate smile he was sure she shared with no one else.

"Let's go and talk with my father."

CHAPTER 9

MARY

Glancing at the line of Nazarene women waiting to use the community well, Mary slipped her arms around the cool clay of the water vessel perched on the stony ledge. Taking a deep breath, she hefted it and stepped back. She walked three steps before a familiar tightening of her abdomen caused her hands to open reflexively

"No!" As the word escaped, her pitcher tumbled to the packed earth and shattered.

Shards of pottery flew in all directions. The freshly drawn water drenched her sandals and the hem of her dress. Mary stumbled backwards and might possibly have tumbled into the well had a steadying hand not gripped her arm firmly.

"Careful, girl!" The woman who had been standing behind her in line turned away, holding her own vessel possessively.

Mary put a hand to her swollen stomach and felt it tighten under her touch. She winced as the contraction intensified, and took in a couple of steadying breaths.

"I'm sorry."

"There is no need for apologies." Rebekah, her neighbor from across the street, gripped Mary's shoulders supportively and glared at the woman angrily. "You've been through pregnancy before, Nava. You know what Mary is going through."

Nava scowled but did not answer. Instead, she turned away from them and bent over the well.

"Are you all right, child?" Rebekah patted Mary's arm as she release her.

Mary nodded as she waited out the contraction. Soon, the pressure eased and Mary found it easier to breathe. Reaching inside her robe pocket, she rubbed a thumb over the wooden rose Joseph had made her months ago. The feel of it comforted her. She habitually placed it into her pocket each and every morning since he gave it to her. Just touching the wooden rose throughout the day calmed her, making Joseph seem closer than his wood shop. When the contraction passed, Mary released the flower.

Gazing down at the shattered vessel, she sighed. She wanted to have Joseph's meal prepared by the time he returned home, but a second trip to the well would delay her. She knew that if she did not hurry, the mutton roasting over her cook fire back at home would burn.

Rebekah offered her own pitcher full of water. "Take mine, Mary. I have a second at home already full. If I need more water, I can always return later."

"Rebekah—" Mary started to say, but her neighbor hushed her.

"You can send it over with Joseph after you have purchased a replacement."

Mary smiled in gratitude. "Thank you."

"Why don't you hurry home? I will pick this up. I am sure your husband will find a use for the shards."

Nodding her appreciation, Mary sucked in a determined breath and hurried forward. Her mind on the meal, she caught herself just before starting down the road that would take her to her father's home. Even after nearly six months of marriage, on occasion she still found herself subconsciously thinking of her father's house as home instead of the place she now lived with Joseph.

Turning in the proper direction, she started walking, but had gone only a few steps when she heard the beginnings of a commotion behind her. Swiveling, she saw that groups of people were beginning to shift toward the center of the small village. *I've still got time,* Mary told herself as her curiosity got the better of her. Setting the full vessel near the wall of a nearby home, she followed a few of her neighbors over to the crowd.

"What is happening?" she asked a farmer by the name of Jarom.

He spat on the ground in disgust. "The filthy Romans want more money is what's happening."

Another man jerked a thumb in the direction of a Roman messenger and the handful of armed soldiers guarding him. "He better be careful to stay with his escort," he growled. To Mary's horror, she could see him fingering a knife in one hand. "I don't imagine he'd want to find himself walking alone along the streets during this visit."

"Easy, Simon," Jarom said, pushing down on the angry man's arm until the dagger was hidden within the folds of his robes. "There is no need for that kind of talk. Besides, what do you think will happen if the soldiers catch wind of your words? Romans don't take kindly to the murder of their citizens."

"One day, Jarom," the man insisted, "the Nazarenes will stand up against the iron fist of the Roman Empire. One day we will drive them from our land."

"You are a fool, Simon," Samuel, a baker with a shop near Joseph's, said with a bitter laugh. "The only thing we'd succeed in doing is decorating a bunch of crosses."

"It is because of cowards like you that—" Simon spluttered, but Jarom took him by the arm and quickly led him away from the gathered crowd.

"Samuel, what is going on?" Mary asked, still slightly unnerved by Simon's angry, rebellious attitude. She had heard Joseph talking about the dissenters, but this was the first time she heard talk of open defiance to the Romans in the streets of Nazareth.

"It is just more Roman bureaucracy," the baker said dismissively. "Emperor Augustus is demanding that every man register as a Roman citizen. Anywhere else, this would mean that the tax collectors would simply circulate around to each of the territories. We, as a people, tend to make things a little more difficult. The roads will be busy in the next week with everyone traveling to their ancestral homes. The innkeepers must be salivating at the prospective business."

Mary felt her face go pale as she placed a hand over her belly. That meant that both she and her husband's families would be forced to journey to the south. Logic told her that Joseph would attempt to leave her here, as Bethlehem was nearly one hundred miles away from Nazareth. Mary knew that should he leave within the next week, he might not have enough time to return before the baby was born. *I will not deliver this baby without him,* she promised herself on the spot, *even if that means going with him all the way to Bethlehem.* Her mind wanted to recoil from the thought of spending five days on the road at this late stage in her pregnancy, but at the same time, she felt a familiar burning within.

"Thank you, Samuel," she said, bowing her head slightly. "I should find Joseph and let him know what is happening."

The man gave a distracted nod.

Mary made a discreet escape, weaving through those still trying to figure out what was going on. Hurrying as quickly as she was able, she returned to Rebekah's pitcher. With effort, she lifted it. When it was cradled once again in her arm, she strode home, unconcerned that some of the water sloshed over the side. As she walked through the front door, Mary could smell the scent of cooked mutton.

I nearly forgot about that! Good thing I was in a hurry. She set the pitcher on the table in front of her and moved to the small cooking fire behind the house so that she might tend to the meat. As her mouth watered at the wonderful smell, she remembered her time spent at the home of Zacharias and Elisabeth and the way that food made her nauseous. She was awfully glad that the sickness portion of her pregnancy had passed. Now, she was simply ravenous … all of the time. It was good that Joseph made a decent living. The money he brought in kept them well stocked and provided for her occasional cravings.

By the time her husband returned, Mary was slicing the mutton into bite-sized chunks and sliding them into the stew she had prepared.

"Mary," he called from the doorway, "I have news!"

"I'm in here, husband," she answered, already sure she knew what he was going to say. "Why don't you wash up, and we can talk over dinner."

A moment later, he poked his handsome face into the room she used for preparing food. Her heartbeat quickened when she glanced up from her work to see him smiling. He still had the ability to take her breath away. She could not believe how fortunate she had been in marrying such a good man. He easily lived up to the promise he made her so many months before.

Working quickly with both of their parents, he organized a small, secluded wedding ceremony. Mary still recalled the covert looks of bitter disappointment Salome had cast in her direction. Joseph's mother had always planned on a large celebration for her son's wedding, and she had been displeased that Joseph decided to keep things simple and private. Even after she and Joseph explained the need for secrecy, Mary was sure that her new mother-in-law blamed her for the rushed wedding.

It had been isolated, but Mary still treasured every second of the ceremony. Somehow the significance of their union struck her as more profound due to the intimacy of the moment. It was something that she would never forget, and now, as she suffered through the final stages of pregnancy, she relied on the memories of that special day more than ever.

With a soft sigh, Mary leaned back and stretched. It was good that they had performed the ceremony when they had. Not long after they wed, Mary's condition began to manifest itself physically. She was now at the point where she could deliver at any time. While the idea of delivering scared her, she wouldn't miss the awkward way her belly pulled on her back with every move she made.

"Is everything all right, my love?" Joseph asked, stepping back into the room just as Mary dumped the meat into the stew. "You are not in pain, I hope."

"I will be fine, beloved," she answered, wiping her hands on her apron.

"That may not be true once you've heard my news, Mary." His serious tone made her uneasy as he entwined her still greasy fingers in his now clean hands. "An edict has come, from Caesar Augustus himself. Caesar wants a census of all Roman subjects. Unfortunately, this means that such a registration take place in our ancestral homeland."

"Bethlehem," Mary whispered, the name of the city causing her stomach to churn.

Joseph dropped his head. "Yes. I've already been to speak with my father and Jacob. We leave in two days. Mary … I …"

Mary steeled herself, mentally preparing the arguments she would make as to why she should not remain behind.

"I feel that you should accompany us," he finished quietly. "I don't know why. I know that it makes no sense. You are so close to delivering the baby, but something keeps telling me that I should keep you close. I already shared my thoughts with our parents. Your father understands, although your mother is justifiably nervous about the journey. My mother thinks that I am crazy to take you all the way down to Bethlehem, now of all times, but I can't deny what I feel."

Mary let out an explosive breath at these words. A relieved grin spread across her lips.

"What is it?" Joseph asked, raising an eyebrow in confusion.

"I was preparing to argue with you about it," Mary confessed. "When I heard about the edict, I felt the exact same way. I promised myself that I wouldn't be left behind. I wasn't at all sure how I was going to convince you. I give thanks that my husband is a wise and faithful man." She lifted a tender hand to her husband's surprised face. "I will be all right, Joseph. I would travel twice as far to avoid being separated from you when the baby is born. Besides, both of our families will be there. I think between Salome and my mother, I will be in good hands."

"It scares me, Mary." Joseph lay a gentle hand over hers. "But the Lord chose you as the handmaid for His Only Begotten for a reason. I will not doubt Him. I am confident that this is truly His will, and He will make you strong."

While grateful her husband welcomed her presence on the journey, Mary was suddenly overcome by worry.

"Joseph," Mary said softly, bowing her head to avoid looking at him, "I am scared to leave. I know that this decision is right, but Nazareth is the only home I have ever known. I am afraid to have this baby so far from here."

He must have sensed her uneasiness. Joseph stepped toward her and cupped her cheeks in his warm, calloused hands. He lifted her chin until her eyes drew level with his. Love and compassion emanated from his touch in waves.

"I think it is time we said a prayer," he replied.

Mary blinked in surprise. Under normal circumstances, Joseph was extremely private and reserved when it came to outward manifestations of his faith, and this unexpected suggestion surprised her.

"I would like that." She stepped into his embrace. The awkwardness of her swollen belly was noticeable between them, but Joseph's powerful arms wrapped around her protectively nonetheless. With a sigh, she rested her head on his chest.

The baby kicked. Excited, Mary reached for her husband's fingers. "Joseph," she said placing his hand on her abdomen. "He is kicking!"

"I love that feeling." Joseph massaged the spot. "There he is! Hello, Jesus. We are very excited for you to get here."

Mary loved it when Joseph spoke to the baby in this way. At first, she worried that a part of him might resent the fact that Jesus was not, in every sense of the word, his. Joseph, however, acted for all the world as though the coming child belonged to him, and Mary's fears had been laid to rest long ago. He was going to make a great father.

"Mary. Mary, wake up."

Mary jolted awake to the feel of Joseph's gentle touch on her shoulder. Reaching up, she rubbed her eyes as she tried to clear away the cobwebs from a restless night of sleep. Though her dreams were already slipping away, a queasy feeling in her belly testified to their unpleasant nature.

"I apologize for rousting you so early, my love," Joseph said quietly, "but we must break our fast quickly this morning. There is much to do for both of us if we are to be prepared to depart tomorrow at daybreak."

With the knowledge that her husband was right, Mary groaned and struggled to sit up. Her back ached from the restless night. She missed being able to sleep on her stomach. Ignoring the pain, she swung her feet off the edge of the bed, wincing when her feet connected with the cold stone floor. Gritting her teeth, she forced back the sickness and stood. The room swam for a moment. She steadied herself by gripping the bedpost until the room slid back into focus.

"Will you be all right, Mary?" Joseph asked in concern, reaching out a steadying arm. "You told me you were no longer experiencing the sickness."

"It will soon pass," she said, closing her eyes against the dizziness. "It is nerves, nothing more."

"Do not overwork yourself," her husband warned. "Take breaks as often as you need them. I will return as soon as I am able to help with the packing."

"Take care of things at the shop first," she replied, pressing a quick kiss to his cheek. "Just give me a moment to change my clothes and clean my teeth, and then I will prepare something for you to eat."

Soon Joseph left for the shop with plans to finish what projects he could. His afternoon would be spent visiting clients to notify them of the need for a delay, something Mary knew he dreaded. It could not be helped. She was glad that he took comfort in the fact that many of the clients must also depart.

The sickness which overtook her when she first woke lingered throughout the morning. Mary was continually forced to pause in her labors and wait for the nausea to pass. Just as she had in the first stages of her pregnancy during her time with Elisabeth, she carried around a bucket just to be safe. Even as she worked, she kept a constant prayer in her heart. The journey loomed larger than ever, and she was having trouble keeping the dread at bay.

Relief arrived around midday in the form of her mother. The moment Anna crossed the threshold to her daughter's new house, she took charge. Without so much as asking, Mary found herself whisked to the nearest chair. Anna quickly soaked a strip of cloth and placed it on her brow.

"Now, stay there, child," Anna scolded when Mary tried to rise, protesting that she should be helping. "Your face was as white as a sheet when I arrived. If you are determined to make this trip, you will need to rely on the help of others. Conserve your strength and just tell me what still needs to be done."

"But Papa—"

"Nonsense, it was your papa who sent me over here. We are all but packed, and Joseph has offered us a portion of his cart for our belongings. Not needing to take two carts will speed up the trip appreciatively. We will journey with you for the majority of the trip, at least until we reach Jerusalem. We will separate from you there. Now, I see that you have already packed the swaddling clothes. Have you considered blankets yet? You can never have too many blankets for a newborn while traveling."

CHAPTER 10

JOSEPH

J oseph, this isn't working." Mary shifted irritably, as though trying to slide down from Saffron, the donkey she rode. "If I keep bouncing around like that, I am going to end up having this baby right here on the road. I need to walk for a while."

Joseph masked a smile with a cough as he hurried to help. He felt terrible about the situation that the census placed his young bride in, but he could not help but find her constant bouts of discomfort amusing at times. It had not taken him long to discover that his wife displayed a tendency toward theatrics when she became annoyed.

"Of course, my love," he answered, gripping her waist as she slid to the ground. "Is there anything I can get for you?"

"I could use a drink of water, if you wouldn't mind. Why does the road have to be so dusty today?"

Joseph pulled a stopper off of his water-skin and handed it over to her.

Jacob stepped up beside them, his walking cane swinging with his shuffling steps.

"Our people are wanderers at heart, daughter," he said philosophically. "Not many of us remain in the same town where we were born. We don't travel near as far now as our ancestors once did, but not many remain in the village of their birth."

"I still think Mary should have stayed in Nazareth," Salome groused from behind them. "She would have been much more comfortable at home."

"Salome." Heli motioned for them all to pause long enough for his wife to catch up. "We are descended from the house of David. Both Jacob and I share this lineage and we are proud of our forefathers. While the Roman, and even the Herodian, authorities would have allowed us to register in Nazareth, Bethlehem is our ancestral home. We have raised Joseph to take pride in his lineage. You know as well as I that he would not disgrace the memory of his ancestors just to try and shortcut something as commonplace as a registration. We taught him better than that. I am positive that Mary would not have allowed him to do so had he suggested it."

"I know, Heli." Salome tucked a strand of loose hair back into the scarf covering her head. "I am just frustrated with the timing of this particular census. I don't want anything to happen to my grandbaby."

"Believe me, Mama," Joseph smiled knowingly, "nothing will happen to this baby. He will be just fine."

"You know, the pair of you are very fortunate to know the sex of the child already." Salome met his smile with a reluctant grin of her own. "The midwife is convinced that you are wrong. She has told me so … multiple times."

"Yes, well, she didn't have access to our source," he answered, winking slyly at his wife.

"Joseph, don't be smug." Weariness dripped from Mary's words as clearly as the sweat and grime from her brow.

"Have you ever been to Bethlehem, my love?" Joseph asked his wife, hoping to distract her from the misery of the dusty road.

Mary looked ahead to where her own parents traveled with the cart. "Father says he took me when I was a baby, but I can't remember it."

"It is a small town." Heli tightened the belt on his traveling robe. "Not much bigger than Nazareth. It is mostly agricultural and pastoral in nature. Sheep roam the land surrounding it, and shepherding is a common occupation there."

"That's not surprising." Mary sucked in a jagged breath and reached for her belly. "What with David being a shepherd. Did..." A grimace twisted her lips.

Joseph reached a steadying hand to her. "What is it?"

"Give me a moment," she said between gritted teeth.

"Mary," Salome said in a soft voice, lifting a hand to wipe a strand of the girl's hair from her cheek, "these contractions are beginning to worry me. Bethlehem is still more than four days away, and the time between your contractions is decreasing. Are you sure you won't ride in the cart?"

Mary shook her head, breathing heavily as the contraction eased. "I thank you for your concern, Salome, but walking really feels best at the moment. I will let Joseph know when I am tired. Heli, would you continue to tell me about Bethlehem? Your words help to take my mind off my pain."

Heli shook his head at Joseph's worried frown. "Of course, child."

Joseph held his hands out to the meager fire, rubbing them together in an attempt to absorb the warmth. *At least Caesar waited until spring,* he thought glumly. *This journey would have been extremely unpleasant otherwise.* Even with the fair weather, he still couldn't believe that he decided to bring Mary along. What *had* he been thinking? She was obviously miserable, and they were still four days away from Bethlehem. They had attached themselves to a caravan of other travelers and while it afforded them additional protection from the dangers of the road, the price they paid was speed. *Although, how much faster could Mary travel?*

"Joseph?" a voice called from the darkness. "Is that you?"

"It is, Jacob," Joseph answered, turning to peer into the darkness. "The fire is not quite dead, if you would like to join me."

His father-in-law materialized out of the darkness. "Thank you. I think I will. Are there any dates left? Anna mentioned that she left them sitting by the fire."

Joseph lifted the small clay bowl next to him and shook it. The dried fruit rattled within. "There seem to be." He held the smooth bowl out in front of him. "Would you like some?"

Jacob approached the fire and sat across from Joseph, and then reached for the bowl. "I would. Thank you, my son." He took a bite of fig and chewed. "How is Mary?"

Joseph sat straighter. "Sleeping, I hope."

"That is good. Are Anna and Salome still attending to her?"

Joseph nodded. "They are. In fact, they kicked me out of the tent. Anna said something about how a wipe down with wet cloths and a change of clothes might help to slow down the contractions."

"Well, Anna would know," Jacob said. "Have you decided whether you want to take the shortcut through Samaria? I know you and Heli were talking about it earlier."

"We were." Joseph slid a stick through the orange coals to stir up a weak flame. "And I still think we need to stay with the main caravan." He pointed to the other fires dotting the road around them. "I've talked with many of the families, and they are all in agreement. Everyone seems to think that the extra distance is a small price to pay to avoid the Samaritans. While I do not necessarily hold with the animosity that most seem to feel for the people of Samaria, I do believe we would be safer to remain with the main group. With all of these travelers, robbers will be salivating for a chance to pick off lone travelers. They shouldn't approach a caravan of this size. Not when we have this many armed men."

In frustration, he stabbed the fire sending sparks flying. He knew that his decision was correct, but the thought of an extra day on the road with his wife in her condition was not pleasant to consider.

"For what it is worth, I agree with your decision. Safety should be the priority," Jacob said, reaching across the fire to pat Joseph on the knee. "While we are on this subject, there is something I feel we should discuss."

"Please," Joseph indicated, motioning with the stick, "continue."

"Well, both Anna and I decided that it would be best if she were to remain with Mary until after the child is born. I know that we originally decided to separate at Jerusalem, at least until after I registered our family, but with Mary's contractions ..."

"Are you certain, Jacob?" Joseph asked. "There is the very real possibility that we could arrive in Bethlehem and Mary will still be several days from delivery."

"I know, but we don't want to take that risk. Salome will need all the help she can get. I can handle the census on my own, and once I am done, I will continue on to Bethlehem and find you."

Joseph nodded. "If you are sure, I know that Anna's support would be most welcome."

"Thank you, Joseph. I am glad that we were able to settle this." He looked up as footsteps approached. "Heli, join us!"

Joseph spun around to see his father standing behind him. "Here, Papa," he said, shifting to the side. "There is plenty of room."

"Why, thank you, Joseph," Heli said with a chuckle, reaching down to lean on his son's shoulder as he lowered himself to the ground. "By Moses' staff, I'm starting to sound like a rusty gate. I am getting too old for these days on the road." He turned to face his son. "Are you still worrying yourself to death about my new daughter-in-law?"

"Is it that obvious?" Joseph asked, hanging his head slightly.

"It was a little better this afternoon," Heli answered, "but you really should try harder. If you are not careful, she will pick up on your nerves. More than anything right now, Mary needs support and positivity from you. She has enough to worry about without adding you to her list."

"I can't help it." Joseph thrust the stick into the center of the fire. It felt good to finally say it out loud. He had contained these feelings all afternoon, trying not to let them show, but he could no longer hold it back. "I see her suffering and there is *nothing* I can do. I feel hopeless. Was I wrong? Perhaps I shouldn't have brought her after all."

For a moment no one answered. Joseph could hear the fire crackling. His stick ignited. The flames leaped around the dried bark.

"Mary is stronger than you think, Joseph," Jacob said, his tone both proud and concerned. "She always has been. I don't know if you would have been able to keep her from coming even you forbade it. Ever since she was young, she has had a mind of her own. If I know my daughter, she would not have allowed you to leave without her."

Joseph leaned closer, enjoying the insights into the mind of his wife.

"Believe me, I worry about her as much as you do. I have lived through the trial of having a wife experience childbirth. Everyone knows that it is not easy for women, but sometimes, I think that we forget how difficult it can be for the men. It is not easy to stand back and watch your wife experience all of that pain, especially the first time. If we were back in Nazareth, I would say that you have a right to fret. In fact, I am sure that my daughter would take offense should you not.

"Unfortunately, we are not in Nazareth. Heli is correct. Mary is very receptive to the emotions of others. She will pick up on your worry if she has not already, and she will suffer for it. Though I know it is unfair to ask it of you, I must add my voice to that of your father's. If at all possible, you must hide your concern from her, at least until after you reach Bethlehem."

Bristling a little at his father-in-law's words, Joseph resigned himself to listen.

"I see that you are doing everything possible for my daughter. You allow her to pick the pace, her manner of travel, and you almost seem to know what she needs before she even asks. Mary knows that you are doing everything you can, my son. Remember she is strong and she knows what she is doing. You are a good man, Joseph, and a suitable husband for my daughter. I am proud to have you for a son-in-law."

Joseph reached up to rub his face with the back of his hand. He was glad that the darkness hid his tearstained cheeks from the two older men. He knew they were right. He had to find a way to do better. Reaching into his pocket, he pulled out a block of wood and a carving knife.

"Thank you for the advice," he said when he felt he gained control over his voice. "I will strive to follow your counsel. The last thing I want is for her to waste energy worrying about me."

He felt his dad's arm wrap around his shoulder. "You are a good son, do you know that?" he said with a chuckle. "Now, did I ever tell you about the time your mother—"

"She is sleeping," Salome said, interrupting her husband as she approached the dying fire. "Joseph, why don't you join her in your tent? Get what sleep you can, but try not to wake her. Heli, are you ready for bed? I am sure I would be *fascinated* to hear the end of the story you were about to tell."

"I just sat down," her husband protested.

Joseph could almost hear his mother's eyes rolling as she looked down at him. Heli must have felt it too, because, grumbling, he pushed himself to his feet. "I suppose I am at that."

"What about you, Jacob?" Anna asked, her voice floating out of the darkness as she approached behind Salome.

"I believe that the time has come for me to retire as well." Jacob offered a friendly smile and rose. "Sleep well, Joseph. Heli, Salome." He tipped his head to them before shuffling off in the direction of his tent.

Joseph watched as they disappeared into the darkness before pushing himself to his feet. After kicking dirt over the last dying coals of the fire, he shuffled back to the tent he shared with Mary. Maybe after such a long and arduous day on the road, she might be able to sleep through the night.

"Mary." Joseph reached out to touch his sleeping wife lightly on the shoulder.

He smiled when her eyelids fluttered open. He enjoyed watching her wake, watching the myriad emotions play across her face. Her expression of bafflement quickly slid away the moment her mind fully engaged as she focused her beautiful blue eyes on him. Absently, she tried to push herself into a sitting position. The awkwardness of her swollen belly had her groaning and flopping back down on the mat.

He watched her roll to her side so that she could gain the leverage necessary to rise. Joseph was once again taken aback by the things he took for granted. He turned away before Mary could catch the pity in his eyes and remind him once again that he should not let her see his worry.

"Is it already time?" she asked, shoving the tangled mass of her hair from her face.

"I'm afraid so. I let you sleep as long as I dared, but many of the other families are already packing their tents."

"Thank you." Mary put a gentle hand on his arm. "You should see to the animals. Saffron seems to be doing all right, but I have noticed that Sage is favoring his right front hoof. You may want to check him before hitching him up to the cart."

"I will take care of it, my love." Joseph reached for the blanket they shared the night previous and winced when he pulled it back, exposing her ankles. "Those already look pretty swollen. Maybe you should start out riding this morning."

"Joseph," Mary said, quirking an eyebrow, "look at me. Everything is swollen! I'll be fine. Just be a dear and help me stand. I need to pack."

"Don't be silly, child," a voice said as a hand pulled back the flap to their tent. Salome pushed her way inside, followed closely by Anna. "Joseph, the morning meal is prepared. Why don't you go out and eat with the men? By the time you are finished, we should be ready in here."

"Thank you." Joseph glanced over at Mary. "Is there anything else you need before I go?"

"No, husband." Mary rolled to her knees. "Go and eat. I will be ready soon enough."

Joseph tucked the blanket he had just folded into one of the packs and stepped toward the opening of the tent.

"Would you like me to brush your hair, Mary?" Salome asked as Anna straightened the rest of the tent.

"Actually, what I really need to do is relieve—"

Joseph pushed his way out of the shelter with an explosive breath. Shaking his head at how blunt women could be with one another, he raised an arm in greeting as his father strode toward him. Seeing the grim determination on the older man's face, Joseph lowered it. Staring over Heli's shoulder, he saw that a few of the people who had been traveling with them were already leaving.

"What's going on, Papa?" he asked, hoping his voice carried more caution than anxiety. "What has happened?"

"It's the caravan, my son. It is splitting up. Many are unsatisfied with the pace we have been traveling." Heli cast a withering look over his shoulder. "Several patriarchs met early this morning and decided that Mary's condition is a detriment to the group."

Joseph's mouth dropped open. "But—"

"They are scared, Joseph. They worry that if we continue at this pace there will be no place to stay once they reach their destinations."

Closing his mouth, Joseph nodded. He knew that Mary was doing the best she could, but the day before he also noticed the amount of travelers that had passed their caravan by.

"We will be all right, my son," Heli hurried on. "There will be many people traveling the roads. What is left of our group is still sufficient to ward off any bandits until we join up with someone else."

Joseph tried to rein in his anger. He supposed that he could understand their sense of urgency, but it was difficult to imagine himself abandoning a woman heavy with child, no matter what the alternatives might be. *But,* he thought, *the group's anxiety is valid.* It was a concern that Joseph found himself worrying about as well. What was going to happen once they arrived? Bethlehem was not a large town. Would it be able to accommodate everyone?

Still feeling deeply uneasy, Joseph walked over to inspect his cart and animals. He bent low over Sage's hooves and began to pick the rocks out. Remembering his wife's warning, he paid particular attention to the front hoof on the donkey's right side. As he lifted it, Sage brayed and tried to pull back.

"Easy, boy," Joseph said in a calm voice, examining the underside of the hoof. It did not take long to discover a sharp rock wedged in there. "I see it," he continued to soothe as he carefully worked the stone free. "There you go, Sage. That should make things easier for you."

"Hi, Joseph," said a quiet voice from behind him.

Joseph released the hoof and turned to see the baker's daughter smiling shyly.

"How are you, Sarah?" he asked, forcing a smile of his own as the young child came up and placed a hand on Sage's flank. "Did you sleep well?"

"The ground was hard," she answered, rubbing her hand on the animal's course coat.

"Yes," he agreed patiently. "It certainly can be."

"Papa said that he would try to find some mats in Jerusalem for our trip home," she continued.

"You know what?" Without thinking it through, Joseph crouched down so that he could meet the child's eyes. "I like sleeping on the hard ground."

"Really?" she asked wrinkling up her nose. "Why?"

Joseph shrugged. "It reminds me of when I was a boy, traveling with my father to sell our woodwork." He dropped his voice to a conspiratorial whisper. "I'll tell you what," he said, glancing around him as though looking for someone that might overhear, "if you promise not to tell all of the other kids, I'll let you have *my* sleeping mat. That way, you won't have to wait until you get to Jerusalem. How does that sound?"

When her eyes lit with excitement, Joseph felt his face relax into a real smile. The next couple of nights might not be the most comfortable, but at least this young child would sleep easier. He could purchase a mat of his own once they reached Bethlehem.

CHAPTER 11

JOSEPH

ver **O** the next few days, Joseph could only watch helplessly as his wife grew ever more pale and listless. He knew she was trying to mask her discomfort and pain, but each time she dismounted from the donkey he could hear her wheezing breaths as she pushed herself harder than she should. It was miserable for her, and Joseph constantly fought his impatience to increase their pace. He wanted to get his wife settled in.

They separated from Jacob at the Jerusalem crossroad after a tearful goodbye and promises that he would find them in Bethlehem. Joseph led Mary, Heli, Anna, and Salome onward. The road was crammed with other pilgrims. At times, the dust was so thick that he could barely breathe. Because their pace was so uneven, they were constantly passed by other travelers and forced to step off to the side of the road until their dust clouds could settle. To say that the conditions were not ideal for travel was a severe understatement in Joseph's mind, but through it all, Mary refused to complain. She worked hard to keep her spirit up.

Joseph's respect and admiration for his wife grew exponentially during their journey.

It wasn't until they were late into the afternoon about a league from Bethlehem that matters escalated. Although the heat was only a fraction of what it would become later in the season, the sun shone brightly, and he could feel the warmth radiating through his clothing. If he were already this hot, he could only imagine how Mary felt with the baby inside her, kicking away. As he led their team of animals with Mary walking next to him, she suddenly cried out in pain and crumpled to the ground, clutching at her protruding belly. He quickly halted the donkeys as Anna and Salome rushed to her side. His mother massaged Mary's stomach gently, murmuring into her ear as Mary clenched her teeth to fight back a scream.

"Joseph," Anna said, glancing up at him worriedly as he fought with the reins to keep the nervous animals from spooking, "she won't last much longer."

"That was the longest one yet," Salome agreed when Mary finally started to relax. "She needs to lie down. We are running out of time."

Taking one look at his wife's flushed cheeks, Joseph nodded.

"I need to get her into town," Joseph said, beginning to unhitch one of the animals.

The cart was unique, designed by Joseph and Heli. Most donkey carts were built for either one animal or two, but not both. Joseph had designed this cart to fit one set of shafts or two, depending on what he desired the animals to do. He unhitched Sage from the cart and handed the reins to his mother. Next, he pulled a pair of iron pins from the shafts, detaching them from the cart. Hefting the shafts, he carried them to the side of the cart and lashed them in place. Once they were secure, he slid the pins out of the second set of shafts and centered them on the cart.

With Heli's help, he guided Saffron into place and secured the shafts in place with the pins.

"Papa," Joseph said, stepping away and taking Sage's reins from Salome, "can you guide Saffron and the cart into the city? She is the stronger of the animals, but the load will still be difficult for her. Mary will ride Sage. Mama—"

"We are coming with you, Joseph," Salome said firmly.

"But—"

"Joseph," Anna said, laying a hand on his arm, "think about how many travelers we have seen on the road today. Bethlehem will be awash with people. What will you do if Mary goes into labor while you are still trying to find a place to stay? We are going to come because our daughter needs us. I appreciate that you are in a hurry, but you must think about what will happen once you arrive."

Not wanting to spend any more time arguing, Joseph shrugged as he leaned down to address his wife. "Mary," he said softly, forcefully slowing his speech and keeping his voice calm, "I know you are in pain, and that the last thing you want to do right now is ride, but ..."

"I understand, Joseph," Mary said through gritted teeth. "Just help me up."

He nodded and dropped down, offering his knee so that she could climb up. "We are only a league out," he soothed. "It shouldn't take us much longer."

"Joseph," Mary growled, wincing as she shifted around on the donkey's back, "you know that I love you, but right now, words of consolation are the last things I want to hear. Let's just get into the city."

"Of ... course, Mary," he said, taking the lead rope.

"All will be well, Joseph," Heli added. "I will take care of our possessions and find you once I arrive. Now, for the sake of my daughter-in-law and my grandson, please make haste."

With a nod, Joseph started out, leaving his father to adjust the cart so that the remaining donkey could more easily handle the load. He started down the road of packed dirt, trying his best to ignore the dust kicked up by the other travelers. Glancing back at his wife, he saw her slouched forward, gripping her belly. Her eyes were closed, and her lips moved soundlessly. Salome and Anna walked on each side of Sage, both resting a supporting hand on Mary. Silently grateful to have the pair of them there, Joseph shook the reins to increase their speed.

Long before they reached the town, Joseph began to see tents popping up all around them. At first they were scattered, but by the time they reached the outskirts of Bethlehem, the canvas shelters were clumped thickly together, as though vying to be closest to the town entrance.

"That can't be a good sign," Mary said quietly, causing Joseph to turn around and look at her.

"What?" he asked, wincing when she sucked in a sharp breath and squeezed her eyes shut.

"Breathe slowly, Mary," Anna soothed. "That's it, the pain will pass, just relax. No, don't push. You aren't ready for that yet. Just breathe."

Joseph hurriedly turned away, blinking back tears as his wife struggled through yet another contraction.

"That," Mary said weakly, once it was over. She motioned to the tents and the gathering of people milling about on the road just inside the town.

"We'll find something," Joseph said with a deep, steadying breath. "We have to. Just stay close. Anna, Salome, keep a tight grip on Mary. It will be difficult to stay together once we reach the crowd."

Just then, four men dressed in plain, sturdy clothing and holding long shepherd's crooks broke away from the waiting mass and made their way toward them.

"Excuse me," Joseph said, hailing them as they passed.

"Yes," answered a man with a thick black beard and a friendly smile. Joseph judged him to be about ten years older than himself.

"Is all of Bethlehem this crowded?" Joseph asked.

"I'm afraid so. The entire town is packed with people coming in for the census. I have never seen this many people around here."

"It is a good time to be heading out into the country," another of the younger shepherds said with a laugh.

"Ishmael, hush," the oldest of the four men said, glancing up at Mary in concern. "Is everything all right here?" he asked.

"Actually," Joseph said trying to keep the feelings of panic and despair from his expression, "my wife is unwell. She is in desperate need of a place to lie down. Do you know of any inns nearby where I could take her?"

The man frowned and reached up to stroke his black beard thoughtfully. With his other hand, he spun his crook in slow circles, the end of it sliding in the dirt as it turned.

"You are very late in arriving, my friend. Bethlehem is ill-equipped to deal with this many people at once. Most of the inns are full to bursting. We saw a great many people preparing beds in the side streets. You will be hard pressed to find any rooms still available. In fact, that is the reason we are on our way out. There isn't enough food in town to feed the new arrivals and I am worried that someone might attempt to steal some of our sheep. Even had you arrived much earlier in the day, you would have found it difficult to find accommodations."

"It couldn't be helped," Salome said impatiently. "We traveled as quickly as we could."

"I understand, my lady," the shepherd said, not unkindly, "but that does not change your situation." He turned his attention to Joseph. "There is a slight chance that you might have luck appealing to the gentler side of one of the innkeepers…"

"I understand," Joseph replied, careful not to look at his wife. "Thank you for your time."

"I am truly sorry, my new friend," the man said with a small bow. "I wish there were something more I could do to help you. I would offer my own house if I could, but my brother's family has already overrun the place. There is hardly room to move inside. May God be with you."

Joseph gave a weary nod and turned back toward the throngs of people. He shook the reins and started the donkey moving. What was he going to do? If what the man said were true, it would be impossible to find a place to stay, let alone somewhere with enough privacy for Mary to deliver the baby.

"Have faith, my husband," Mary said quietly from the back of Sage. "Don't forget what you told me before we left. The Lord will provide for us."

"I know, but …" Joseph began, but the words faded away when he realized he did not know what to say. His worries continuing to gnaw at him, he reached up and ran a hand across his parched lips. For the first time in hours, Joseph realized how thirsty he was.

"My love," he started to ask, reaching for the water skin tied to his side, "are you—"

A tug on his robes interrupted him. He turned around, not wanting to give a pickpocket the chance to find the purse hidden in his robes. Instead he found himself looking into the earnest face of the younger shepherd.

"I know you are in a hurry," the boy called Ishmael said quickly, casting a quick glance at Mary before turning away again with a blush, "but there might be another way ... if you cannot find a room, I mean. My father runs an inn on the other side of town, near the southwest entrance called the Sheep's Head Inn. It is already full, but maybe there might be something he can do to help. Anyway," his head shifted to eye his departing companions, "I have to go or Amos will leave me behind. Just tell the innkeeper that Ishmael sent you."

"Thank you, Ishmael," Joseph said gratefully. "If we can't find something else first, I will take your advice."

The young shepherd bowed. "Good luck to you and your lady." With that, he turned and hurried after his companion.

Not wanting to waste any more time, Joseph joined the group of people shuffling into the city. He scanned the buildings searching for a place that they might stay. The first inn was just to his right, but he saw a hastily scrawled piece of parchment nailed to the door stating that it was full.

"Joseph," his mother demanded as he stared at the untidy handwriting, "what are you doing?"

"It is full," he said, thinking that perhaps she could not read the sign. "We need to keep looking."

"I can see that it is full," she growled, glaring as though she caught him playing in a mud puddle in new Sabbath day robes. "Your wife is heavy with child and suffering. Get over there and ask if they have enough room for her!"

Starting guiltily, Joseph glanced up to where Mary sat sidesaddle on the donkey. She still appeared as though she was seconds away from passing out, but upon hearing Salome's firm tone she gave him a tiny smile. Approaching the structure, Joseph lifted his arm and rapped on the door. At first, no one answered, but just as he lifted his hand to knock again, the door cracked open and an elderly woman's face peered out at him.

"We are full," she huffed, jabbing a meaty finger at the posted sign.

She made as if to shut the door, but Joseph stuck his foot in front of it to keep it from closing.

"Please, my wife is with child. She is about to del—"

"No room here," the woman said again. Putting her weight on the door, she managed to shove it closed.

"There is another just up there," Anna supplied helpfully, pointing to where a man leaned against a doorway, watching the crowd of people with a wistful expression on his face.

Joseph walked over to him, but the man began to shake his head even before Joseph could open his mouth.

"I have no room left," he said sadly. "There is barely enough room to walk in there. I have mats spread out over every cubit of floor inside. That's why I am out here, to be honest."

"But, my wife," Joseph started to protest, "she is in a lot of pa—"

"I'm sorry, young man. I would help you if I could. It kills me to have to turn people away. You wouldn't believe how much money I have been offered if I could just make a little more space, but it makes no difference. I can't offer what isn't there."

"I understand," Joseph said, trying to mask his disappointment. "Thank you." He spun back to see his wife folding inward on the donkey, with Anna and Salome on each side trying to keep her balanced as she fought the pain. His panic increased. There had to be something he could do. People crowded all around them, some of them approaching the same innkeeper who had just turned him away. Many cast sympathetic looks in Mary's direction, but nobody stopped. The noise in the small town seemed to crescendo as his nerves spiked. He wanted to cup his hands over his ears to tune it out. Instead, he shook the reins and started them forward again, having no idea where he would go.

Just before he reentered the crowd of people pushing toward the center of town, an elderly woman caught his attention. She waved at him from under the shelter of a canopy. It appeared that she had been selling fresh fruit, but her stands were completely empty. A small basket lay overturned in front of one of the stands, and hundreds of pits were scattered over the ground. Not knowing what else to do, Joseph threaded through the crowds, earning many dark looks as people were forced to walk around Sage's bulky body.

"You seem to be in some distress, young man," the woman said, raising a hand in greeting.

"It's my wife," Joseph began, "she—"

"I have eyes, boy. I wish I could tell you that I have room for you to stay, but my house is full of children, grandchildren, and a handful of great grandchildren. However," she continued, motioning behind her, "I have a bench in the shade. It isn't much, but, I daresay it will be more comfortable than the back of that donkey. Perhaps your wife could rest here while you continue your search for accommodations."

Joseph thought this sounded like a wonderful idea, but he didn't want to speak for Mary. Instead, he turned to glance over his shoulder. Both Salome and Anna nodded vigorously.

With an appreciative nod, he motioned them forward. "Thank you so much for your offer." He handed the reins of Sage to his mother. "Please take care of Mary. I will move much faster by myself. Perhaps there is something available further in. It is only natural that these inns would fill up first."

Salome lifted a hand to pat his cheek. "Of course, my son. Don't be long. This rest might help us slow the contractions temporarily, but we really need a place where we can prepare her for the birthing."

Nodding, Joseph reached up to help Mary down from the donkey. Gingerly, she slid down from the blankets covering his back. Feeling himself suddenly free of his burden, Sage lowered his head to sample the fruit pits strewn about his feet.

"Hold on just a little longer, my love. I will find something soon," Joseph said, guiding Mary over to the sheltered bench.

"I will be all right, Joseph," she said giving him the small, private smile that she reserved just for him. "Hurry back."

"Of course," Joseph answered, leaning down to plant a kiss upon her brow, "as soon as I possibly can." He turned to the fruit vendor. "Thank you. You cannot know what this means to us."

"I have experienced childbirth, young man," she said airily, waving him off. "I am confident that I understand what she is going through a lot more than you. Now hadn't you better get going?"

Joseph reached into his pocket, pulled out a small coin and held it out to her. "Thank you for the generosity."

The woman gave him a disgusted look and pushed the hand away. "Don't insult me, boy. I have done nothing more than simple decency would have me do. Now go."

With a nod, Joseph closed his fist over the coin and turned away from the fruit stall. For the next hour or so, Joseph jogged from house to house, in the end not even caring if they were inns or not, but he couldn't find room anywhere. A handful of innkeepers offered him a bit of space where he could toss down a sleeping mat, but the moment they discovered that he was accompanied by a wife near delivery, the offer was rescinded. He worked his way down the main street in Bethlehem and turned down many of the side streets before he finally found himself standing in front of a shabby building with a sign stating that it was the Sheep's Head Inn.

Wearily, Joseph flipped the coin he still held in his hand, catching it so that the edge of the metal stuck out between his second and third fingers and knocked on the coarse wood. After a moment, he heard a shuffling sound behind it and tentatively, the door opened.

"The inn is full," a gruff voice said. "We've no room left. You should have come earlier in the week."

"Please," Joseph said desperately, "I met a young man heading out to the fields by the name of Ishmael. He pointed out your inn to me. He said it was possible that you might be able to help me."

"Why?" the innkeeper asked suspiciously. "What has that foolish boy committed me to? How are you different from the countless others who have come through here seeking refuge that I have already turned away?"

"Not me," Joseph pleaded, "my wife. She is with child, very close to delivery, and I am running out of time and options. Please, isn't there anything you can do?"

The door opened another few inches. Joseph held his breath, watching as a rough, grizzled man scratched at his beard.

"You should have thought this out more thoroughly, boy. This is a bad time for a woman with child to be traveling."

"Are you married, sir? Perhaps you know of some secret to making a woman do what you want when they have already decided to do something else."

For the first time, the innkeeper smiled. "No, indeed, I have discovered no such secret. Come with me, young man. I think that I may have a place that just might work for you." He stepped the rest of the way through the door. "Hannah, care for our guests. I will not be gone long!"

CHAPTER 12

MARY

Mary arched her back against the pain and bit down on the scream that wanted to escape. "Please, God," she whispered as soon as she caught her breath, "help me to endure this pain."

"Deep, slow breaths, child," Salome said for the hundredth time. Mary gritted her teeth to keep from saying something she knew she would instantly regret. As had been her habit during most of her contractions, she reached in and gripped the ornamental rose tightly. Feeling the polished wood in her hand, she breathed easier. As she calmed, the door opened behind them, and Dinah, the elderly fruit vendor, descended from the steps of her home.

"How is she?" she asked, holding out three clay cups.

Again, Mary found herself guarding her tongue. The pain and constant aches frayed at her temper. She knew the woman meant well, but she was tired of people speaking for her and acting as though she were not there.

"The contractions have slowed somewhat," Anna answered, gripping Mary's hand tightly, as though reading her daughter's irritation. "This respite was exactly what she needed."

"I am glad it has helped," Dinah said, pouring water into each of the cups. "Now, drink. I am sure that handsome husband of yours will be back soon."

"Look, there's Heli!" Salome said, pointing. "Heli! Over here!"

"I'll fetch him," Anna said, wincing at Salome's shrill call. "There should still be a little time before the next contraction."

Mary watched her mother hurry over to the laden cart pulled by Saffron. Heli was struggling with the stubborn creature, and Mary could clearly see that the donkey was exhausted. Even through her own pain, she felt sorry for Saffron. She was pulling a cart much too heavy for her.

More than a few people grumbled when Heli changed directions to follow Anna over to where Mary and Salome sat, leading Saffron behind him. Sage brayed at Saffron when he caught sight of the other donkey, causing Saffron to respond in kind.

"Where is Joseph?" Heli asked curiously, halting the animal in front of them.

"He is searching for a place to stay," Mary answered.

"And you, Mary? How are you feeling?"

"A little better now. Sitting has helped a lot. I am very grateful for Dinah's compassion."

"As are we all," Salome agreed.

Mary sat back and listened as her mother and in-laws continued to chat, trying not to resent the fact that Joseph had not yet returned. The contractions continued to hit, taking her breath away with the sharp pain and pressure. The desire to push against them was almost unbearable, and it was only by listening to the constant murmuring of Anna and Salome that she resisted the urge. Finally, Anna pointed through the crowd.

"Look! I think that is Joseph!"

"Well, finally," Salome muttered, standing and brushing at her robes.

Ignoring her mother-in-law, Mary struggled to regain her feet. Joseph strode purposefully toward them, threading expertly through the milling crowd. Mary watched him approach, and judging from the serious cast to her husband's face, she tried to mentally prepare herself for what would undoubtedly be bad news. There was still room in the countryside to pitch a tent. Perhaps someone could direct them to a practicing midwife to assist with the birth. She tried not to think of the embarrassment of giving birth in a tent, surrounded by strangers.

"Did you find anything, son?" Heli asked, stroking Sage's neck.

Instead of answering, Joseph walked straight up to his wife. "How are you feeling?" he asked, worry etched all over his young face. "You still look pale."

Love filled Mary. Even now, with everything going on around them, Joseph's initial thoughts were for her. "I am fine, my beloved. The baby is coming, but I am prepared, one way or the other. I know God will provide for and protect me."

"I have found a place for us," Joseph said slowly. "It is not a room, but at least it will afford us a bit of privacy."

"Well, then," Salome said hurriedly, "what are you waiting for, Joseph? Lead on! Mary needs to lie down."

"Do we want to hitch up Sage first?" Heli asked. "I don't know how much further Saffron will go on her own."

"Let's do it quickly," Joseph said, beginning to untie Sage's lead rope from the vendor cart it had been hitched to. He handed the reins to Heli before removing the second harness from the cart. As Heli fitted Sage into his harness, Mary watched Joseph worked quickly to reposition the shafts and secure the animals to the cart.

Just as they finished, Mary felt the next contraction coming on. As Joseph tried to guide her to Saffron, sharp pains stabbed through her abdomen. Before she could think of trying to muffle the sound, a cry of agony escaped her lips. Bending over as much as she could, Mary wrapped both arms around her belly and sobbed. Never before in her life had she ever experienced agony such as this. Distantly, she could feel Salome's and Anna's hands gently massaging her shoulders and stomach, but it did nothing to take away the pain. Shutting her eyes, Mary felt the tears squeeze through her lashes and slide down her cheeks. She rocked with the pain and waited for the worst of it to pass. After what felt like ages, she slowly righted herself. Leaning heavily on Joseph, Mary hobbled the rest of the way to where Saffron waited. It took both her husband and Heli to help her mount the donkey, but the moment she felt secure, they started out.

Turning around, Mary waved at Dinah. Although her vision was still blurry with pain and tears, Mary thought she could see the elderly fruit vendor's soft look of compassion.

"Thank you for everything," Mary called.

"Go and have that baby, child," Dinah answered back with a big smile. "May God be with you!"

Turning back, a sudden onset of vertigo seized Mary. She would have fallen if Salome had not quickly pressed against her with both hands until she could once again find her balance. Joseph led them quickly through the crowded streets, pushing through loitering people and offering hurried apologies without stopping. Mary kept expecting him to pull off in front of one of the many buildings, but Joseph did not. He led them past the last of the homes and in the direction of the countryside on the far side of the city. More than once, she wanted to ask him where they were going, but it took all of her energy to keep from sliding off Saffron's back.

Finally, he slowed his pace in a section of town separated from the rest by crudely built wooden fences. Inside, Mary saw cattle, sheep, and other livestock milling around and eating the tall grass. The fences did not follow straight lines, but appeared to her as though the builders had been simply trying to stay ahead of the animals in an effort to contain them. They meandered up the gentle rise of a hill before disappearing on the far side.

"Joseph," she started to ask, "what—"

"All will be made clear shortly, Mary," he said. She caught a note of sadness in his voice. "It is the best I could do, and to be honest, we are lucky to have found it."

He led them along the fence until they reached the base of the hill. Baffled, Mary scanned the rough grass, wondering what on earth her husband was talking about. The road they followed was little more than a dirt track with weeds growing all around it. Wheel ruts threaded through the middle of the uneven trail and Mary was pleased that Saffron opted to walk between them rather than attempt to balance atop the dirt.

Upon rounding the hill, a gust of wind beat at them. Mary lifted the sleeve of her robe to her nose in an effort to block the stench. *Not now,* she begged silently as her stomach threatened to empty itself. Gritting her teeth, she forced down the bile, wishing that she had something to wash down the sour aftertaste it left in her throat. Having been unable to eat much that morning, Mary knew that if she lost the little nourishment she now held, she would become nauseous and would undoubtedly add a headache to the long list of problems she currently experienced.

On the far side of the hill, she saw a small stable built directly into a rocky overhang about halfway up the mound. Sections of the wood in the old structure rotted away, but the hay covering the ground seemed fresh enough. Now realizing exactly what Joseph meant with his vague comments, Mary tried to fight back a wave of disappointment. As though to emphasize exactly where she was, a cow lowed in a long, distinctive baritone before dropping its head once more to graze. The sounds of the animals were all at once deafening to her, and she could hear the short staccato cries of the sheep breaking through the calls of the cattle.

Closing her eyes to the sight in front of her, Mary fought for control. *This is no one's fault,* she told herself fiercely. *At least I will not be surrounded by strange people when I deliver the baby.* Catching a movement from within the shadows of the stable, Mary squinted until she could make out the figure of a tall man busily piling straw together. He looked to be about the age of her own father, and the sight of him sent a pang of sadness through her. She wished that Jacob could be here for the birth of her child. The tall man must have sensed their presence because he hurriedly turned to face them, raising himself to his full height.

"So you are back," he said to Joseph through a heavy dark beard with gray patches. "I am glad to see that I haven't been wasting my time." He turned his attention to Mary and his expression softened. "Hello, child, my name is Jonathan. I am the innkeeper of the Sheep's Head. I believe that you have already met my son, Ishmael."

"We have," Mary confirmed, noting the compassion in the man's voice. "He was very kind."

"He's a good boy," Jonathan said with a nod, before leaning over to dust off his legs. "I am very sorry about the accommodations, but this is honestly all I have left. I have given up every square inch in my inn, including my own sleeping quarters. I hope that the stable will at least grant you a measure of privacy."

"It will be fine, Jonathan." Anna strode forward. "Thank you so much for your generosity."

"Hmph," he muttered, blushing slightly, "Not much in the way of generosity. It is little enough, but all that I have is here for you. I took the liberty of sending one of my daughters out for a midwife. She should be here soon."

"Jonathan," Mary heard Joseph say as she struggled to dismount from Saffron's back. "We have yet to settle accounts for the use of your stable."

Jonathan opened his mouth, but his eyes fixed on Mary for a long moment before he slowly shook his head. "There will be no accounts to settle," he said. "There is something about your young wife, my friend. I get the most peculiar feeling when I look upon her countenance. It is almost ..." His voice faded as once more he shook his head. "I must return to my inn. Please send for me if you have need of something else. I ... wish I could offer you something better."

With that, he turned and strode back toward the more crowded part of town. Mary watched him go for a moment, grateful that he rounded the corner before the all-too-familiar, gut-wrenching pain took her breath away once more. As she prepared for yet another contraction, Mary was vaguely aware of movement around her.

"Joseph," she heard Salome say, "help your father unload the cart. We need the tent. I think we can rig it up to partition a portion of the stable for use as a makeshift birthing tent. Heli, find the bedding and spread it out over that pile of straw. Anna, help Mary through this contraction. Let's try to have things set up for the midwife by the time she gets here. I'll start a fire and get some water boiling."

Even as the pain intensified, Mary felt gratitude for Salome's willingness to take charge and give directions. While her mother-in-law's tendency to take control occasionally pushed the boundaries of Mary's patience, Mary could see that her husband and Heli reacted instinctively to Salome's orders. Leaning heavily on her mother's shoulder, Mary staggered around the outside of the stable as the men worked frantically around her.

"Anna," Heli called from behind a piece of canvas that Joseph was busy stretching across the opening to the stable, "the bedding is ready."

"Thank you," Anna answered, lifting a piece of the thick tent material and guiding her underneath it. "Come on, Mary, you really should lie down."

Wincing in pain, Mary sat heavily on the bed of straw.

"Here," Anna said, wadding up an unused blanket, "rest now, my child."

Nodding wearily, Mary leaned her head back with a sigh. For the first time since arriving to Bethlehem, she felt herself relax. Having been there for Elisabeth's pregnancy, Mary had an idea of what to expect, but she wanted to take this moment at least to refocus her thoughts. She was about to give birth to the Son of God, the child who would one day grow up to save all men from their sins. Although the birth and the implications of Jesus' entry into the world of men loomed large in her thoughts, at that moment, Mary couldn't wait to greet her newborn baby.

"Come on, little one," she crooned softly, affectionately touching her belly. "Don't keep me waiting much longer. I'm too excited to see you."

CHAPTER 13

ISHMAEL

Seated next to his tent, Ishmael gazed out over the hillside at the dozens of sheep grazing below him. While his eyes watched the wandering animals, his thoughts rested on the young couple he had met at the edge of town. He hoped they found a place to stay. With a wince, he shifted his position in an effort to break down some of the sharper stalks of grass poking him in the backside. His crook rested on his knees in front of him, and he fiddled with it absently as he scanned the surroundings for anything that might threaten the animals under his protection.

A sling and a small pile of stones rested next to him. He reached down and ran a hand over the sling's rough leather. It was well polished, and the supple leather rippled under his caress. He practiced with it every day, but rarely found the opportunity to use it while working. Wolves had long since grown either too timid to attack the flocks or too wily to show themselves in the open.

"Ishmael! Jeremiah! Josiah!" Amos called from the small one-man tent he had just finished erecting. "We need to count the sheep. David reported two-hundred and sixty-three before heading back into town. Let's verify his count before settling in for the evening."

Ishmael reached out with the curved end of his crook and wrapped it around the root of a large piece of sagebrush. With a grunt, he pulled himself to his feet and then reached down to grip his sling. He tucked a handful of rocks into one of the pockets of his robe.

A final glance at his tent revealed his blanket poking through the opening. With a sandaled foot, he gently nudged it back in. *Last thing I need is a bed full of bugs,* he thought as he strode toward Amos' tent.

Like it or not, Amos had been placed in charge of the small group of shepherds, and Ishmael and the others had implicit instructions to do as the man ordered. When Ishmael approached, Amos ran a hand through the thick curls of his dark beard. Masking a scowl, Ishmael averted his eyes. Amos knew perfectly well he was sensitive about his own scraggly chin hairs. The older man often teased Ishmael about his lack of facial hair.

It isn't my fault, Ishmael thought as he used his crook to push aside some of the thicker stalks of grass in front him, *I've been growing this thing my whole life. Perhaps God has cursed me with a thin beard.*

As though reading Ishmael's inner envy, Amos flashed a tiny smile and exaggerated the gesture. In an effort to dismiss the jealousy, Ishmael lifted a hand and scanned the horizon. The sun had begun to set, and if they did not hurry, it would be dark before they finished their count. With the sheep scattered all over the hillside—if Ishmael knew Amos—it would be Jeremiah, Josiah, and himself doing the actual count since "someone would have to keep an eye on the camp."

Sure enough, as soon as the other two finished setting up their tents, Amos divided the hill into three sections and sent them marching down.

"Quit grumbling, Josiah," Ishmael called to his friend once he was reasonably certain Amos was out of earshot. "Jeremiah has most of the sheep in his section."

"Shh," Josiah hissed.

Ishmael suspected the sour look on Josiah's face was his effort to keep the count. With a mischievous grin, Ishmael marked the location of the ewe he was on and slowed his pace.

Josiah, his boyish face tight with concentration, focused on the animals in front of him and did not notice. He continued down the mountain with his finger dancing from sheep to sheep as he mumbled to himself. Ishmael pulled one of the stones from his pocket and tucked it in the sling.

Casting a careful glance behind him, he saw Amos' feet sticking out from his tent as he busied himself with something inside. Slipping his finger through the tiny finger loop at the end of one of the cords, he gripped the knotted end tightly in his hand and twirled it in a tight arc. Taking aim, he released the knotted end and let the stone fly. Josiah yelped in surprise and pain as the stone struck him smartly on the backside. Spinning around, he glared at Ishmael who hooted with laughter.

Shaggy white heads lifted as the surrounding sheep studied Josiah. Ishmael tried to muffle the sound, but a single look at the offended expression on Josiah's face made that impossible.

"What is going on down there?" Amos called from the top.

"Nothing, Amos!" Ishmael wheezed, trying to catch his breath. "We'll be done soon!"

"What do you mean, 'nothing?'" Josiah shot back. "You made me lose count. I am going to have to start over now! If Amos catches us messing around, he will find some way to make our night miserable."

"Oh, come on, Josiah," Ishmael said with a chortle, "even you have to admit that was a good shot. Do you think I am as thick as these sheep? Of course I made sure that Amos wasn't watching. Let me finish my count, and when we get to the bottom, I'll help you with yours on the way back up."

"I'm sure what you meant to say was that you will do it *for* me," Josiah grumbled, massaging his rear as he stepped over to join Ishmael, "and that would have been much funnier if you had done it to Jeremiah."

"To you, maybe." Ishmael located the last sheep he had tallied and picked up the count.

By the time they arrived back at the top of the hill, the last rays of sunlight flirted with the darkening sky. Their total was off by seven, and Amos pulled out a tiny quill and piece of parchment to note the discrepancy. "We will try again tomorrow morning." He scowled at the figures on the parchment. "Hopefully your count is simply off, because if not, Jonathan is going to be extremely angry."

"We might get a more accurate tally if you came down to help," Josiah muttered under his breath, glaring at the older shepherd.

Amos either didn't hear or pretended not to, because he continued talking as though there had been no interruption. "Since there are so many people out there tonight, we will double up the night watch. It will mean less sleep, but with potential thieves about, it is our job to protect the sheep. Keep your slings close and your eyes open." Flicking his eyes at Ishmael, Amos' beard quivered. "Ishmael, I noticed that you and Josiah seemed to have a lot of energy. Why don't both of you take the first watch? Jeremiah and I will relieve you when the time comes."

Ishmael winced and glanced down at his sandals. He could feel Josiah's accusing eyes on him along with Amos' smug smile. The old goat had sharper eyes than Ishmael gave him credit for. He would have to find some time to apologize later that evening.

Long after Amos and Jeremiah retired, Ishmael and Josiah sat back to back in the darkness, scanning the hills for possible threats to the sheep. The night was alive with starlight and for some reason Ishmael was having a difficult time focusing on his duties.

"Is it just me," Josiah said curiously, pointing upwards, "or does that star seem brighter than usual?"

There was no need for Ishmael to ask which star he meant.

Right over their heads, a star winked merrily in the night. Ishmael noticed it too. The star had always been slightly brighter than its companions, but tonight it appeared to be spreading more light than usual. Raising his head to study the star, Ishmael jumped when one of the lambs bumped its cold nose into his hand. Sill staring up into the night sky, he scratched the gentle creature under the chin.

"I do believe you are right. How strange. Why would it look different tonight?"

"That's a question for a smarter man than I," Josiah answered. "You never did tell me why you turned back to talk to that man."

Ishmael shrugged uncomfortably. "I am not sure why I did. I suppose there was something about his desperation that struck me. I mean, over the last week, we have seen a lot of anxious families. Some have brought food with them, and a few of those who traveled farther thought to bring shelter, but many simply expected to find a place to stay within the city. What they didn't consider is that Bethlehem really isn't all that big. Papa says that the markets are sold out of most of the wares, and the food prices are becoming increasingly expensive. Shopkeepers are scrambling to find more, but the demand far outweighs the supply. When I heard the man talking to Amos, I felt … something. I am not sure I can describe it. Then when I saw his wife—"

He cut off when Josiah elbowed him in the ribs. "She was pretty, wasn't she? I get it. You saw a pretty face and wanted to help her out."

"No," Ishmael shook his head as a slow flush crept up his neck, "that wasn't it … I mean, yes, she was beautiful, but there was something else about her. Somehow I just felt that I needed to do what I could to help them out. I don't know if Papa can do anything for them, but … I had to try."

Josiah chuckled. "If I know your father, I am sure he managed to do something for them."

"I suppose," Ishmael said with a sigh, "but I—" Suddenly he cocked his head to the side and peered into the night. "Did you hear that?"

"Hear what? Is one of the lambs try—"

Ishmael shook his head. "No, it was … singing. Wait, there it is again!"

"You must be hearing things because … Oh! Yes, there it is! I can hear it, too. What is it?"

"I don't know. I can't even be sure where it is coming from. What are they singing? I can't understand—"

"Ish-Ishmael! Look!"

Hearing the tremble in his friend's voice, Ishmael turned to see Josiah's mouth open and slack as he pointed at the same bright star that had intrigued them moments ago.

Slowly, he rose to his feet. The light, that had been nothing more than an oddity before, now pulsated rhythmically, growing with increased brightness. Ishmael opened his mouth to say something, but a feeling of power and majesty flooded through him. Completely overwhelmed by the bright light and the beautiful singing, he did not turn at the sound of a rustling in one of the tents behind him.

"What in Abraham's name are you two—" Amos started.

"Amos, is it time already? I thought we still—" Jeremiah began, but he too went silent.

Ishmael cringed as the vocals swelled in tempo and volume. Shielding his eyes from the brilliance of the light, he sank to the ground. The light penetrated through closed eyelids. *Am I going to die? Is this what death feels like?* H cowered on the ground and covered his head with his hands.

All at once, the overpowering light dimmed as quickly as it started. The joyful chorus decrescendoed until it was little more than a murmur of sound.

"Fear not: for behold, I bring you good tidings of great joy, which shall be to all people," a pleasant, male, baritone voice said over the singing.

Hesitantly, Ishmael opened one eye. A bearded man dressed in long, white robes stood in the air before them. He held his hands up as if to assure them that he meant no harm. "For unto you is born this day in the city of David a Saviour, which is Christ the Lord."

Ishmael shook his head in awe. *The Savior? How is that possible? He was born tonight?* The woman he had seen earlier…*Was she the mother of the Savior?* Ishmael pushed down the flood of questions filling his mind. Whatever was happening, he knew that he did not want to miss a single word of what this holy messenger was saying.

"And this shall be a sign unto you: Ye shall find a babe wrapped in swaddling clothes, lying in a manger."

With this pronouncement a multitude of heavenly beings appeared behind the messenger, and as one, their voices joined together in song. The unearthly chorus swelled, and this time Ishmael understood the words.

"It's beautiful!" Amos whispered.

Ishmael nodded, tears rolling down his cheeks. "I've never felt anything like this before."

"It can only be the power of God," Josiah agreed. "Did you hear what he said? The Savior was born tonight! Right here in Bethlehem!"

Once more, the chorus swelled, causing all of the shepherds to fall silent as they listened to the beautiful music. The power of their song echoed throughout the hill country. The joyous song of praise and adulation continued. Ishmael knew, in that moment, he could be content for the rest of his life to simply stay and listen to this angelic song.

How long he and his companions knelt there, transfixed as they listened to the music, Ishmael could not say. It seemed like an eternity, it seemed like a second. He only came back to himself when he realized that the angelic choir held out one final, glorious note. His mouth opened with the rest of the angels, the corners of the messenger's lips turned upward in a smile brimming with so much love and joy that Ishmael wanted to weep with happiness.

Then all at once, the song was over. Ishmael blinked in surprise and when his eyes opened, the messenger and his heavenly choir were gone. The night was once more as it had been.

The moon shown overhead and the stars winked with the same merry light as they had before the vision ... or whatever it had been. As Ishmael shook his head, he couldn't help but feel the pain of loss. He ached to hear even a small portion of the song that was rapidly fading from his mind. If pressed, he would not have been able to recall the complex harmonies that filled him so utterly only moments ago. Everything began to fade until only a phrase in the song played over and over in his head.

Glory to God in the highest, and on earth peace, good will toward men.

"I don't think I will ever again witness anything to compare with that," Amos whispered reverently.

Ishmael nodded in agreement, only now noticing that his mouth felt completely dry. He reached down for his water skin and, pulling the stopper, he took a long draw.

"Amos," Josiah said quietly, "I have to go down there. I have to see. That messenger said that ... the savior of the world is down there."

"I know," Amos answered. "I think we should all go."

"What of the sheep? Jeremiah asked tentatively. "Is it wise to leave the sheep alone?"

"It is a matter of priority, Jeremiah," Amos answered. "An angel of God just descended from heaven and told us that the Savior of the world has been born this night. There is a reason he came to us. I don't yet understand what that is, but I think that we are meant to seek out this babe and honor him. I believe that we have been called as witnesses and I intend to fulfill that calling."

Always before, Ishmael viewed Amos with a mixture of jealousy and distaste. Now, after hearing the words of conviction from the older shepherd, Ishmael felt his respect and admiration for the man grow. His greatest desire at that moment was to kneel in front of this holy infant and pay tribute. Then, as though something urged him to hurry, he remembered what the messenger had said.

"And this shall be a sign unto you: Ye shall find a babe wrapped in swaddling clothes, lying in a manger."

Swaddling clothes and lying in a manger, he thought to himself over and over again. Then he understood. Ishmael started down the hillside in the direction of the town.

"Ishmael! Where are you going?" Josiah called after him.

Ishmael didn't take the time to turn around. "Follow me!" he answered, continuing to take long, ground-eating strides toward the base of the hill. "I know where he is!"

CHAPTER 14

JOSEPH

Joseph paced restlessly at the front of the stable. The animals they had cleared out of the shelter scattered all around him. Many of them acted skittish from Mary's cries of pain as she delivered. Those particular beasts, he made sure to avoid.

He wanted to burst through the curtain and take his wife in his arms to assure himself that everything was all right. The screams and cries he had heard from the opposite side of the curtain only moments ago terrified him. It took the combined efforts of himself and Heli to keep the beasts from breaking through the closed gate and stampeding down the road. He could still hear Mary's sobs as she fought through the pain. The after-effects of his dread lingered. His blood had chilled the moment her cries cut off.

On this side of the canvas wall, Heli sat on a bench with his eyes closed and leaned his head against one of the wooden walls. Through the thick material, Joseph could hear the soft, comforting murmur of women's voices.

For what felt like hours and hours, though it could not have been more than a heartbeat or two, quiet filled the stable. His hands trembled as he waited for the sound he longed to hear. Finally, as though it had only been waiting for his attention, the cries of a newborn baby broke through the tense silence.

Then, the cooing of the women began. From that moment on, Joseph stayed near the canvas hoping to hear some news of his wife, but he could not make out anything over the sound of the cries of both the infant and the animals.

"You are going to wear a hole in the ground if you don't calm yourself," Heli commented dryly from his seat. "Sit down, Joseph. Anna and your mother have everything under control."

Joseph tried to heed his father's advice and took a seat next to the older man. After a few seconds, he stood to pace again.

"Joseph," Salome's voice said from the other side of the curtain.

"What is it, Mama?" he asked, rushing over to her.

"No, don't come back yet," she said, gripping the canvas and holding it closed. "Anna and I are cleaning up. Mary and the baby are fine. The midwife is applying oil to both mother and child as we speak. When we are finished, we will take this down. I am sure that the night air will do Mary some good. For now, however, we need something to lay Jesus in once he is wrapped. Mary is still too weak to hold him without assistance."

Joseph looked around wildly, ecstatic to finally be of some use. His eyes settled on Saffron and Sage. The two donkeys ate from a wooden manger lined with a cloth sack and filled with grain.

"I have an idea," Joseph said, struck by inspiration. He dashed over to the crude feeder and gently pushed the heads of his animals away. Reaching in, he pulled out the sack full of grain and set it at their feet. Quickly, he stuffed the manger with fresh hay and bent to lift it. The wood creaked ominously. He set it back down, afraid it might come apart in his hands. The feeder was of a basic make, with four legs secured to a box made of wooden planks. The base was narrow and widened toward the top. Staring at the poorly made manger, Joseph itched to have it in his shop so that he might clean it up.

"Joseph," Salome called, "what are you doing?"

Shaking his head to clear it, Joseph shook the manger experimentally. Although he knew that he would never have dared to sell something so poorly made, it would serve the purpose he had in mind.

"I'm sorry, Papa," he said regretfully, "but I need your help."

With a sigh, Heli opened one eye. "What is it, Joseph?"

Joseph pointed to the manger. "Mama said they need something to lay the baby in. I think this will work, but if I try to carry it myself, it is going to fall apart. We need to grip it from the legs to keep it together."

Heli grunted as he stood. Approaching the manger, he studied it with a practiced eye. "You know, you made better pieces of woodwork than this when you were ten years old."

"Heli," Salome said with a warning note in her voice.

Recognizing the tone, Joseph and Heli both bent down and gripped the legs. Lifting together, they hoisted the manger.

"You go first, Joseph," Heli said with a grin. "An old man shouldn't have to walk backwards."

"Of course, Papa," Joseph answered, walking slowly toward the opening past the curtain that Salome held for them.

The soft, flickering light of burning lamps lit the cool dark room, but even with the muted flames, it felt dark and closed in.

"I see what you mean, Mama," he said as he walked past her. "You could definitely use a little air in here. May I see my wife?"

"If you are quiet," Anna said, rising from a bed of straw in the middle of the room. "She is resting, but I think it would be a comfort to her to have you near."

"Joseph?" Mary said weakly, raising a hand toward him. "Have you seen him? He is the most beautiful baby I have ever seen. His eyes are as blue as the sky."

"Where do you want this?" Joseph asked, trying to keep the impatience out of his voice. He wanted to go to his wife's side.

"Set the bed over by the canvas," the midwife ordered from the ground behind where Mary lay.

Glancing over at her, Joseph could see a rosy pink arm waving about.

"Yes, that is a good boy," the woman murmured. "Now, you hold still and let me finish this wrap."

When the baby cooed, happy tears welled in Joseph's eyes. Hurriedly, he led his father over to where the midwife had instructed and set down the manger. After giving it a couple of shakes to make sure it was secure, he reached out for a clean piece of cloth and tucked it around the hay to give the child an extra layer of protection from the sharp ends of the dry grass. When he was satisfied, he strode over to Mary.

"Hello, my love," he said softly. "How are you feeling?"

"Do you want the honest truth?" she asked with a wan smile. Dark bruises circled her exhausted eyes, and she was still pale and shivering.

Reaching out, Joseph tucked the blanket up and under her chin. In her hand, she clutched the wooden rose he had made for her. The sight of it sent a strange combination of pride and guilt running through him. He still wished he could take back the harsh words he spoke to her upon her return trip from Hebron.

He pushed away the bad memory so he could focus on his wife. "I'm not quite sure how to answer that."

"You are supposed to tell me how beautiful I look," she teased, entwining her hand in his.

"That goes without saying." Unable to resist her never-failing sense of humor, Joseph chuckled. "You are always beautiful to me, Mary."

"You are telling stories, my husband," she answered, humor dancing in her tired eyes. "I look like I just wrestled three escaping ewes."

"Then you are the most beautiful ewe-wrestler there ever was."

"She was very brave, Joseph," Anna said proudly. "She will be a strong mother to baby Jesus."

"Come over here, Papa," the midwife interrupted, grinning at Joseph. "You should greet your son."

Mary squeezed his hand. "Hold him, Joseph. It is like nothing I have ever experienced. When those big blue eyes stare up into yours ... well, you need to see for yourself. Go on, I'll be right here."

Feeling his hands tremble, Joseph balled them into fists and straightened. His heart beat rapidly as he stepped over to the midwife. "You are sure he will be all right?" he asked dubiously. "I don't want to hurt him."

"Don't be silly," she answered, smiling as she rose. "Babies love to be held. Just cradle your arms and give his head the proper support. I've already wrapped him up, so he is warm and comfortable." Gently, she lowered the infant into Joseph's arms and stepped back.

For the first time, Joseph gazed down into the perfect face of the boy he would call his own. He might not be the child's literal father, but in that instant, he knew that he would do anything for this baby. He would love him as if he were his own flesh-and-blood son.

Warmth enveloped Joseph as he cradled the infant, and once again, he felt the hot sting of tears as they slid down his cheeks and into his beard. This boy was the savior of the world. The literal Son of God. This tiny child was destined to save all of mankind.

How can I possibly be worthy to raise this child? Jesus blinked and peered into Joseph's face. Joseph felt as though those tiny blue sapphires saw through his own eyes and directly into his soul. Doubts immediately rose to the surface. All at once, he was keenly aware of his imperfections. How on earth could he hope to be an example to this child? What could *he* possibly teach the child that would prepare him for so great a calling?

Suddenly, not quite trusting himself even to hold this precious gift that God had seen fit to grant the world, Joseph walked over to the manger and gently lay the boy down. Wrapping a tiny blanket around the baby, Joseph leaned down and kissed Jesus on the forehead. As he did so, a feeling of comfort flooded through him.

Not quite ready to face his wife and family, he began to pick at the knots tying the canvas to the walls of the stable. As he worked to take down the covering, Joseph's attention constantly strayed to the tiny child lying comfortably in the manger.

"The time has come for me to return home," the midwife said, gathering up her tools and medicines. Tucking a U-shaped stool under her arm, she waved at Mary. "Send someone if you need anything, child. Remember what I told you about feeding him. He will need to eat very soon."

"I will remember. Thank you so much for your assistance."

"Master Heli? Are you coming? Why don't you, Salome, and Anna accompany me home? It is a bit late for a woman to walk the streets of a crowded town alone. Besides, it will give our new Mama and Papa some time together."

"That sounds like a wonderful idea," said Heli, holding his hand out for his wife. "Anna, would you care to join us?"

"Oh," said Anna, the worry evident in her tone. She cast a nervous glance at her daughter.

"I will be fine, Mama," Mary assured her. "Joseph will help me with anything I might need. You said yourself that there wasn't much more that we could do tonight. Go out and get some fresh air."

"Very well, my daughter. We won't be gone for long."

"Ah," Mary said when everyone left and it was only the two of them, the baby … and the animals. "That is so much better. Thank you for opening the covering. It really does feel good to see the stars again."

"You are welcome. Is there anything else that I can get for you?"

"Well, you could come and put your arms around me," she said seriously. "That would be nice."

Grinning and shaking his head at the audacity of his wife, Joseph returned to her side, and just as she had requested, he lowered himself to the hay and gingerly wrapped his arms around her. She winced slightly, but when he tried to pull his arms away, she linked her hands with his and held them in place.

"It isn't you. Everything feels achy and sore right now, so if I am going to feel that way anyway, I might as well have you close."

"Of course, my love."

"So," she asked after a comfortable minute of silence. "Did you feel it?"

"Feel what?" Joseph whispered into her ear.

"Did you feel the way Jesus looked at you?"

Joseph shrugged uneasily. "I've never felt anything quite like it."

"I *told* you so! Isn't he adorable? I have to admit, he is the most beautiful thing I've ever seen."

"Well." Joseph ran a hand down her back and leaned in to kiss her. "The second most beautiful."

"Excuse us," a familiar voice said.

"Yes?" Joseph asked in a cautious tone, rising quickly to his feet. "Who is there?"

A discreet distance from the stable stood four outlines. "We have come to see the child that will one day be the savior of the world."

The speaker was young. Joseph thought he recognized the voice, but he had spoken with so many people that day that he could not place the owner. He drew himself to his fullest height, determined to protect his precious family. "How did you come by that information?"

"Please, sir, certain things are too sacred to be shouted out in the open. We are all unarmed. You have my oath that we will bring no harm to you and your family. We have simply come to witness the miracle of the Christ child."

"Joseph," Mary said softly, "let them come. They won't hurt us. I think they are the shepherds we met upon entering the city. If that is true, we owe them our gratitude."

"Come forward," Joseph called with the briefest of nods.

The men shuffled in slowly. Joseph studied them as they stepped into the flickering lamplight. It was just as his wife had said.

"Look," one of them whispered, awe evident in his voice as they stopped before the manger where Jesus lay. "That must be him!"

"Just like the angel said," another breathed.

"Ishmael, isn't it?" Joseph greeted. "And Amos."

"Well met, my friend," Amos said warmly, his eyes lifting from the tiny bundle. "Congratulations on the birth of such a beautiful baby."

"I'm glad my father found a place for you," Ishmael added, smiling shyly, "but I'm sorry it was in the stable."

"Ishmael," Joseph said warmly, "we owe you and your father a great deal. This was more than we could have hoped for." He reached out across the manger and placed a hand on the young shepherd's shoulder. "My name is Joseph. That," he pointed to where his wife lay, "is my wife Mary, and this, as you already seem to know, is Jesus."

He reached under the blanket and delicately picked up the sleeping child. "Please enter. I believe there are some milking stools over there. We would love to hear your story … if you have time, that is."

He walked over to Mary and, upon seeing the eager gleam in her tired eyes, he squatted down and transferred Jesus into her waiting arms.

Ishmael smiled at the family. "It is a deep honor to meet all of you. You already know Amos and me, and these other two are Jeremiah and Josiah. We watch over my father's flocks."

"We can't stay long, Ishmael," Amos warned, though his eyes were glued to the baby in Mary's arms. "The sheep are unattended."

Ishmael nodded. "I understand, Amos, but Mary and Joseph should know. What if the angel visited others as well? Joseph and his family could end up with more unexpected visitors."

"I'm confused," Joseph said. "What angel are you talking about?"

"Joseph," Mary said, rolling her eyes as she stroked the baby's face tenderly, "isn't it obvious? How do you think they knew that

Jesus was born? You will have to excuse my husband. He has had a long day."

"Not so long as yours, my love." Joseph turned to the shepherds. "So Gabriel came to see you, too?"

"We don't know," Amos answered. "The angel didn't give us his name. He simply told us about your baby. Once he finished delivering his message, Ishmael led us here."

"Come now, Amos," the shepherd Ishmael had introduced as Josiah demanded, "that is all you mean to tell them?" He gave a dismissive shake of his head to Amos and turned his attention to Mary and Joseph. "We were up in the hill country, just outside the town. Ishmael and I were watching the flocks and talking when he mentioned that he hoped the pair of you had found a place to stay. Just after that, we noticed that one of the stars seemed brighter than the others. Right before our eyes, the light intensified, and then we heard the music. I can honestly tell you it was the most beautiful song I've ever heard."

"It was faint at first," Ishmael said, taking up the account, "but it grew louder. An angel appeared and he told us that a savior had been born this night and that we would find him wrapped in swaddling clothes, lying in a manger."

"Don't forget about the angel choir!" Jeremiah shook his shepherd crook with a reverent enthusiasm. "They appeared behind him and sang songs of praise about your baby's birth."

"Then, all at once, everyone disappeared." Josiah hurried to add his voice to the story. "Although the star still looked slightly brighter than the others, everything else was the same as it had been before."

"It was the most wonderful feeling." Amos paused, his features softening. "All of us were in agreement. We wanted to come and see what the angel was talking about for ourselves.

Since Ishmael seemed to know exactly where you were, we followed him here."

Joseph studied Ishmael. "How did you know?"

"It was strange," he said, blushing slightly. "When the angel said that the babe would be in a manger, I knew exactly where my father had taken you."

"We are sorry to intrude on so beautiful a moment," Jeremiah said, "but we could not pass up the opportunity to see the savior of the world. What a magnificent thing. What an incredible experience to see him with my own eyes."

"I want to tell everyone," Josiah agreed, his eyes shining with excitement. "Everyone should know about this."

The shepherds visited for quite some time. When Heli, Salome, and Anna returned, perhaps an hour later, the men once again shared their vision. The second telling included some of the smaller details which escaped them in the grandeur of their initial excitement at being in the presence of the man who would one day save the world.

After a few not-so-subtle hints from Salome, Amos clued in to Mary's exhaustion. The younger men wanted to stay, but the older shepherd insisted they depart and give the family a chance to rest.

They departed in high spirits, vowing to share the miracle with all they came into contact with. Joseph noticed the zealous glint in Ishmael's eyes in particular. There could be no doubt of the boy's convictions. With a sigh, Joseph realized that if they were to stay for more than a couple of days the stable might well be overrun with visitors.

Once the company departed, Mary fed the baby. Even as she nursed, Joseph watched as her eyes continually drooped before jerking back open. It did not take long for the child to finish, and after a bit of haggling, Joseph convinced his wife to release her grip on Jesus so she could sleep. He gently carried the babe back to the manger, set him inside, and tucked a blanket around the small child.

Satisfied that the infant would sleep soundly, he helped his father lay out the rest of the mats so everyone would have a place to rest for the remainder of the night. There was a bit of fussing from the two women about holding the baby, but Heli, from his bedroll, pointed out that there would be plenty of time for it tomorrow and that dawn could not be far away.

Grateful for his father, Joseph dropped heavily onto his own mat and pulled his blanket up around him. Peace and happiness spread through him. As his eyes slid closed, Joseph's thoughts lingered on Jesus.

EPILOGUE

MARY

n the early hours of morning, Mary was wakened by the cry of her child. Rubbing her eyes, she pushed herself into a sitting position. Sleepily, she turned her attention to the manger where her baby now stirred.

"I'll get him, Mary," her mother said softly, pushing back her own blanket. "He is simply hungry."

"Thank you, Mama,." Remembering how often Elisabeth's baby wanted to eat, Mary nodded. "I think you are right."

Glancing down, she saw her wooden rose lying next to her. She must have fallen asleep while holding it. Lovingly, she picked up the token of Joseph's affection and tucked it into a lower pocket in her robes for safekeeping.

"Do you want something to lean against while you feed him?"

Mary tried to scoot forward on the mat and winced in pain. "That would be wonderful. I could also use a little more light, if you wouldn't mind."

"I'll take care of it."

Her mother expertly handled Jesus in one hand, bouncing him softly while making hushing sounds. She carried a milking stool over to where Mary sat and pushed it against her back. Then, as Mary situated herself, Anna poured more oil into the lamps that had burned low while continuing to comfort the whimpering babe. By the time Mary was prepared to receive the child, lamplight flickered merrily in the still semi-dark stable.

"Do you need anything else?" Her mother bent and laid the baby in Mary's cradled arms.

The moment Jesus was placed in her care, he stopped fussing. Mary smiled when she saw his tiny mouth began to root for nourishment. *So small, and yet he already knows his mother.*

"I will be fine," Mary assured. "Get some sleep, Mama."

"I am right here if you need anything," Anna said, placing a comforting hand on Mary's shoulder. "Don't hesitate, child."

"I won't, Mama. Thank you."

Anna crawled back under her blankets as Mary held the tiny child close and considered all that had happened in the past few months. She had experienced a myriad of highs and lows, from exquisite joy to crushing sadness and everything in between.

Now, she sat here, in a stable of all places, nursing the savior of the world. She already ached for the child, instinctively knowing that Jesus' predestined calling would be difficult for him and all those who loved him. Yet, she also knew that this tiny infant would one day bring a peace and joy to all those who believed in him.

What a blessing it was to be chosen to bring him into the world of man.

"I will do everything I can to raise you right, my son," she whispered softly. "I love you more than I ever knew was possible. I am so glad you are finally here."

Mary sat still long after Jesus finished eating and fell asleep. She lifted him to her shoulder and patted his back, watching as the light of day slowly chased away the stars.

Even while those around her slept, Mary ran through the long list of miracles that had happened in so short a time, from the initial visit of Gabriel to the birth of John, from Joseph's change of heart to the coming of her son. She considered the shepherds' account of what happened to them in the hill country.

Something within Mary told her that the miracles were far from over.

Jesus stirred in her arms. Beaming down at her son, Mary was filled with joy and love. She gazed into his sleeping face, an undefinable emotion burning within her.

Soon, her husband and family would wake. Another day would begin. A part of Mary ached to share her thoughts and revelations with them. Another part whispered assurance that there would be time for discussion later. In this moment, she was not quite ready to lay her musings bare.

For now, at least, she kept them *and pondered them in her heart.*

The End

ABOUT THE AUTHOR

J.R. Simmons lives in Northern Utah with his beautiful wife and four handsome boys. Although fantasy and adventure usually fill his mind, he can't quite settle on a single genre. He has dabbled in historical fiction, mythology, and even children's literature. He enjoys writing simply for the sake of story creation. He also likes performing. Whether it is acting, singing, presenting, or reading aloud, he loves to be in front of a crowd. He is an avid gamer, movie watcher, and electronics fanatic. When he is not exercising the right side of his brain, he enjoys participating in triathlons and playing sports with his kids. Most nights he can be found either sitting down with a good game, a fun movie, or huddled over his computer writing.

Connect with J.R. Simmons
Facebook: http://www.facebook.com/authorjrsimmons
Website: http://www.magicunleashedbooks.com/
Twitter: jrsimmons_3

BOOKS BY J.R. SIMMONS

RAGESONG SERIES

Ragesong: Awakening
Ragesong: Uprising
Ragesong: Retribution
Ragesong: Alliance
Ragesong: Triumphant

THE GATES OF ATLANTIS

Madness Behind the Throne

CHILDREN'S BOOKS

Yay, Zombies!

OTHER BOOKS

Lo, How a Rose: The Nativity Story